MOTHER AND DAUGHTER

*An unputdownable psychological
thriller with a breathtaking twist*

James Caine

PROLOGUE

Before

Mother says we're helping the children in the basement. Sometimes it doesn't feel that way.

When I hear their small voices and the others crying, some asking for help, I wonder if Mother is right.

"Ms. Annie Meadows!" Mother calls out to me from the kitchen. I stand from the living room table.

"Yes," I say as I approach her cautiously.

She's standing over the stove, a spatula firmly in her hand. She nods her head towards a plate of food.

"If you would, my darling child," she says to me with a smile, "please, give this to room one."

"Okay, Mother," I say, giving her my own smile back.

She raises the spatula. "And," she says, "do not speak to room two. You promised me you would stop. I know you did last night."

How did she know? I wasn't loud. They were scared and lonely. They needed someone to talk to. I like to think I help people too, better than Mother does.

I continue to stare up at my mother, and the spatula over her head. Her smile fades. "Now, little girl, please do as I say. Hurry, before their food gets cold. And—"

"I won't speak to them," I complete her sentence for her.

"Good," she says. "Now, after lunch, we're going to start our reading period."

I grab the plate and start walking down the narrow basement stairs.

I love reading. I love learning.

Sometimes I wish I could be more like the other children I see from my bedroom window. When Mother gets ready for the day, I watch the kids scurry down the block to get to school on time. On nice days, Mother allows me to read outside on the porch, where I can hear the sounds of nearby schoolchildren playing outside at recess.

They'll yell and scream their heads off for some reason, and I wonder what could be happening to them.

I hear yelling from the basement, but it's different.

Mother teaches me at home. She tells me I'm smarter this way. I'm special. Not like the other children. I have a deeper purpose than the children I hear outside.

Sometimes though, I wish I was just like the other kids. I wish I could scream with them from the playground.

One time I asked my mother if I could go to school like the other children.

She did not like that question.

She said it was important for us to stay home. What we did with the people in the basement was special.

Nobody but us could do it.

Mother made me promise to never tell a soul what she does. They wouldn't understand. They wouldn't see it as helping the children.

Mother says that after they leave our home, they're different. Better.

Changed.

We're making them whole again.

I've never seen the children after they leave to ask, but I wish I could. I want to know how much better their lives are. I want to know how happy they are after staying with us.

I want to tell the voice inside me that questions Mother that what I help her do is helping them.

As I get to the basement, I hear muffled sounds coming from one of the rooms. I walk past a bookshelf, where we hide the hole that leads to the special hallway where we keep them.

Inside are two rooms. Each has a heavy door that Mother has to help me unlock and open.

Both rooms have a metal slot at the bottom of the door. I open it, and place the plate of food inside room one.

"Thank you," a little girl's voice says.

I do as Mother asks and don't speak to them. She's likely upstairs listening. She's likely testing me to see if I'll do as she asked.

I may be only seven years old, but I know to follow what Mother says.

I close the slot and look down the small hallway at room two. The muffled sounds continue to come from it.

The sounds of crying.

Mother says we're helping them. It doesn't feel that way.

CHAPTER 1

Sarah
Present

Report Domestic Abuse.

I stare at the signage in my doctor's office as I wait in the lobby for my prescription.

I think of my husband, Roger. Last night was not a good one. This morning too. I wish I could go back in time and stop our fight from getting worse.

De-escalate Roger and get him to cool off before he exploded.

Worse, it all happened in front of Gracie. She's only four years old but knows that daddy gets angry sometimes.

It scared her. She doesn't understand. She doesn't see what led up to our fight. I took things too far. I should have backed off, knowing that Roger was going to be upset.

Instead, I made things worse. I yelled at him. Said things I regret.

Roger didn't like that. His voice started to raise and match mine, and soon after he was flat-out yelling.

Things got worse.

It was only when I saw the frightened face of my little girl that I worried about it.

I saw my father and mother fight when I was young.

That was as normal as Tuesday coming after Monday. Father would yell, but unlike me, my mother just took it. She never did so much as whimper back to him. That didn't stop my father from starting arguments.

Father was a shorter man. Not really intimidating for his size. Even as a child, I thought he was frail. I would yell back at him continuously. Rebel child, my mother called me.

Not her. She was the complete opposite. Fully submissive.

Whatever my dad said, she did. Whatever Father commanded, she followed.

At least Roger is different. He certainly is many things, but he's not like my dad. That much I got right when I married him.

The fight last night bothers me, though. I wonder what Gracie is thinking. What her little mind is construing to make sense of it all.

I sigh, and the doctor comes into the small waiting room. "Hey, Sarah," she says with a smile. "Sorry for the wait. Our printer stopped working and I had to use my non-existent tech skills to fix it to print this off." She hands me the prescription. "I know you're worried about the side effects of taking Prozac, but I know this will help things. It's also a very low dose. We can put you on this medication to help, okay?"

I look around the empty room and sigh, knowing that nobody, not even the receptionist who's not at her desk, heard what the doctor said. I don't want to take drugs. My doctor says I have depression. It doesn't feel that way. I still can be with my child and take care of the house. Sure, I'm more tired, but I can still live my life every day.

Functional depression, my doctor calls it.

I grab the prescription and thank her again before leaving.

I'm not sure if I'll actually get the prescription filled. My doctor talked me into taking it from her after reviewing how it could help me. She didn't exactly pressure me, but she didn't exactly let me say no.

I didn't come to her clinic for depression. We were just to review a recent ultrasound I had. Somehow I came for the test on my shoulder and walked out with a prescription for Prozac.

How did that happen?

I take out my phone and notice the time.

I hurry to my car and start it, knowing I'll be late picking up Gracie from daycare again.

Last time the office said they would charge me if I continued to be late. Maybe I can tell them I have functional depression and to give me a break, but somehow I know that won't make things better. Besides, I'd rather not tell anyone.

The supervisor of the daycare, an older lady named Mabel, explained it was just policy to start charging per minute parents are late picking up their children.

That would be great.

Roger would certainly be happier having to pay extra for me being late picking up our child. Especially since he never wanted her to be in daycare to begin with. He'd rather I take care of her at home.

Being with other children at her age is important, though. She needs more than just me or Grandma to play with. Now that I want to go back to a job, we can hopefully afford it.

Thankfully, living in a smaller city has its perks. It's easy to get to anywhere quickly. Esta is the one of the smallest cities in the province of Alberta, Canada.

It has that small town appeal, but with a Walmart.

I park in the lot of a strip mall. When I get out, I can still hear some of the children playing from the gated area where the daycare is.

Their voices make me smile, knowing I can't be too late if other children are there.

I slow and see two little girls playing hopscotch behind the gated area. They're having fun, laughing almost in unison.

Gracie is standing in the corner, alone. She's not doing anything as far as I can tell but look at the brick wall of the daycare. She kicks a stone and watches it fly past the gate.

I wish she would play with other children. She reminds me so much of myself when I was younger. I tended to be alone. Not much has changed now that I'm an adult. I never really had many friends, even in high school. A few, enough to get by, but I had always thought Gracie would be better.

I had hoped she wouldn't be like me.

How could she be any more outgoing with me as her mother?

It's not like we take her out to friends' homes so she can play with their children. Roger and I don't go out often. We're always together, as a family.

We call it family time, and we love having it, but I wish we had more friends. I've heard it's easier to make friends as parents. You bring your child somewhere and if they start playing with other kids, you chat with their parents. Just as easily as your child has made a new friend, so have you.

What if your child stays to themselves though? What

if the child's parents aren't outgoing either? I'm not. At least Roger is very different.

Why couldn't Gracie have taken after him more?

I worry how Gracie will be when she starts kindergarten next year. I remember how it felt playing alone at recess when I was her age. I remember how shy I was. How much I wanted other kids to ask me to play, and how scared I was to approach other kids to play with them.

Gracie's face lights up when she spots me. "Mommy!" she calls out. She puts her hands on the gate and shakes it as if she has the strength to break through.

"Hey, Gracie," I say with my own wide smile. "Did you have a good day?"

"Can we go home?" she asks, ignoring the question.

"Hey, Mrs. Bradshaw." My daughter's daycare teacher, Annie Meadows, walks up to me. Her flowing dress moves wildly with the breeze. I notice the small cartoon hearts printed at the bottom of it. She always has some type of weird dress like that. Gracie tells me what Ms. Meadows wore at daycare whenever I ask her how her day was at home.

Annie pats Gracie's head. "Gracie had a great day today," she says in her usual polite voice.

"Hey, Annie," I say. "That's great to hear." I look down at Gracie. "Can me and Ms. Meadows talk for a moment, dear? Maybe go play on the swing."

Gracie nods and is about to leave when Annie kneels so that she's at eye level with my daughter.

"Please give me and your mother a minute," she says to Annie, repeating what I had just asked Gracie to do. It slightly irritates me but it's hard to stay mad at such an odd young woman.

All the children love Ms. Meadows at daycare; she has a way with them. Gracie always tells me stories about what she did that day. She comes off so awkward and proper to me, though.

Gracie runs towards the swing and sits on it, looking back up at me. "Mommy, can you push me?"

I smile. "I just need a minute to talk to Ms. Meadows, okay? Just swing yourself."

"Is everything okay, Ms. Bradshaw?" Annie asks.

"Please, just call me Sarah," I remind her. I've said it so many times, but Annie is not one to skip formalities.

"Mommy!" Gracie yells, sitting on the swing, not moving, "I don't know how."

I sigh. "Honey, just give me one minute, okay?"

Gracie pouts and sits on the swing, not moving, except to sway a little under gravity.

"Sorry," I say to Annie. I look back at Gracie a moment before continuing. "I'm just worried about her."

"What about?"

"I worry that she's not playing with other children as much as she should."

Annie gives a thin smile. "Gracie is an exceptional child. You really are a lucky mother."

"Thanks, Annie." I smile. "She is, I know. I just worry that she doesn't show much interest in speaking to other children, let alone playing with them."

Annie nods. "I understand. Every child comes into their own social time when it makes sense for them. I'm not worried about her. I was like her when I was younger myself. I had a hard time playing with children, but now I play with them all day."

I smile, but her answer is strange. "Thanks, Annie, I'm sure I'm worried about nothing."

I call Gracie to come and leave with me, and thank Annie again before we do. My daughter holds my hand as we walk into the parking lot.

When we're close to my car, I see several young girls playing at the playground across the street.

I smile while looking down at my daughter. "Hey, I have an idea. How about we play at the playground for a little while?"

Gracie looks across the street, at the children playing, but doesn't answer.

"Come on," I say. "It'll be fun." I point at the empty swing set. "I'll push you this time." Gracie smiles and nods in agreement.

Before I start to push her, I quickly text Roger to let him know that we're at the park beside the daycare.

Gracie and I are having fun, mostly because of my hard labor pushing her. After what feels like an eternity, I stop and tell Gracie that Mommy needs a break.

"Can we just go home now?" she asks.

I look at the three little girls playing near the slide, and the two mothers sitting across from them chatting to each other.

"How about you play for a little more on the slide for a bit? Then, I promise we'll go home." Gracie doesn't seem enthralled. "And if you have fun playing, we'll have ice cream after dinner today!"

That does the trick. Gracie smiles and runs towards the slide where the other children are playing. Instead of talking to them, though, she pours rocks down the slide, making it so the other kids can't go down. I roll my eyes.

I remind Gracie to play nice since others want to use the slide too. One of the two mothers on the bench smiles at me and waves.

I smile back. "Hi," I say to them. Only one of them greets me back.

I go back to the bench I was sitting at across from the mothers and watch Gracie play. After a while, a miracle happens. Gracie is actually talking to one of the little girls at the playground. Soon enough, she joins the others in playing. They sit together on the playground rocks, talking amongst themselves.

I smile. I need to do more of this with Gracie.

She's actually getting along with other children. I think about approaching the other mothers and introducing myself. I can't help but think how one of them didn't greet me back. Maybe they want to be left alone.

As I watch Gracie play with the kids, though, I wonder if I should say something. Isn't this the part where I speak to the children's parents? Ask them questions? Maybe even a number to arrange for a playdate?

Or is that weird?

It all seems so forward.

Before I can make up my mind, I spot my husband's red car coming down the block and parking on the street.

CHAPTER 2

Roger

I stare at the different colored flower bouquets. Which one best represents how crappy a person I feel right now?

Which type of flower tells my wife how sorry I am for last night?

What can I give her so she'll forget the man I was yesterday and remember how I usually am?

A woman who works at the grocery store sees me looking at the flower selection, completely lost. "Can I help you?" she asks.

I take in a breath. She's a young pretty girl. Maybe only nineteen. I remember at her age I used to buy flowers for pretty girls all the time. It was something I charmed them with that they were not used to.

I liked to think that I had "game," as the kids call it these days. A way with women where I could romanticize them into my arms. Flowers always set a nice standard for what they could expect from me.

Now, I'm getting older. I married a pretty girl but haven't given her flowers in a long time.

All I've given her is grief.

"Well," I tell the young woman, "I'm sort of in the doghouse with my wife."

She laughs. "You did have the look of trouble, so I wondered."

I nod with a thin smile. "If I upset you beyond belief, which flowers would you want to receive that could make it so you hate me just a smidge less?"

She shakes her head. "I don't know what your wife likes. Does she have a preference?"

Good question. I don't remember buying her anything in over a decade. I remember when I was younger, I used to know which color represented what emotion. Red was a little too sexy for an apology flower. Implied romance or lust. Not what Sarah likely had in mind for me tonight.

I need a flower that says I'm raising the white flag. I come in peace. I'm not here to fight, and I surrender.

I look at some pretty light pink roses. "You know what, I'll just grab these ones," I say confidently. The cashier nods and wraps them up for me.

When I get to my car, my phone vibrates. I put the bouquet on top of my car and look. It's Sarah letting me know she's at the playground near the daycare.

I don't want to wait for Sarah and Gracie to come back home to tell her how sorry I am. Maybe a visit to the park with my family is the perfect set-up. A good way to reunite with my wife and daughter after last night.

I haven't had a chance to talk to Gracie since my little blow-up yesterday.

I get inside my car and turn on the ignition. It starts as quickly as my rage the other day.

What hurts me most when I think of it is the look on Gracie's face. I remember having that look myself as a boy. Mom and Dad would fight, only he would take things too far.

The first time he struck my mom, I wanted to kill him. Had I not been seven years old, I would have tried. I remember, when my parents were asleep, I snuck into the kitchen and opened the drawer, taking out a large kitchen knife.

He hurt my mom. He was the one who needed to be hurt. What had she done to deserve his wrath? I don't even remember now that I'm an adult. All I do remember was holding that knife, thinking what I should do to him.

It was crazy, I know. I wanted to protect my mom, even if it was from my own father. That wasn't the last time he hit her. It was only when I got older that I challenged him once.

We fought, and I won.

I remember how good it felt, standing over my dad, collapsed on the floor after I smashed him in the face.

He understood who the new man of the house was.

It was better for Mom after that. I'm not sure what changed inside my father, but he never hit her again.

We continued to act as a family, despite our past. We didn't have very many loving times. Eventually I moved out, and he passed away. Mother now lives in a small apartment a few hours away from Esta. We visit her when we can.

It's only been a few months since my dad died. I know I should give myself a break about what happened last night with Sarah. I'm not myself.

My father's funeral wasn't too long ago. As much as I tell myself I don't care about that, I do. It's... complicated.

Still, the look on Gracie's little face gets to me.

I continue to drive to the playground, wondering how I'm ever going to make things up not only to my wife, but my daughter as well.

I look at the bouquet in the passenger seat.

How many times did my father attempt to make things right after he destroyed something?

Never.

How many flowers did he buy my mom?

None.

I'm not him, I remind myself.

I take responsibility for what I've done, and we'll make this right.

How do I make right what I haven't told her yet, though? What will Sarah's reaction be when I tell her I've been lying to her? When she finds out what I've been up to, how many flowers can I buy her to make up for that?

She'll find out eventually, most likely soon.

I can't keep hiding it.

One battle at a time, I remind myself. I have to get through this before I can tell her everything.

I sigh, wondering, what have I done? I'm not myself, though. I haven't been making good decisions lately.

We've had darker moments than this. Six months ago, I thought she would leave me for sure. She should have.

I would have if I were her.

She didn't, though, and things did get better, until recently.

I spot the playground ahead and smile, noticing Gracie playing with other kids. Sarah and I have been worried about her social skills. I've continued to tell her not to worry about it. She'll get more exposure to other kids as she continues with daycare and starts grade school.

Seeing Gracie play makes me smile.

When I park on the street beside the playground, I see

the look of concern Sarah has as she glances at me.

My smile fades as I remember what a piece of garbage I really am.

CHAPTER 3
Sarah

Roger gets out of his car and quickly hides a bouquet of pink roses behind his back, a large smile on his face. I shake my head and smile back. When Gracie spots him, she stops playing for a moment and looks at me.

"My two favorite girls," he says as he gets closer. He reveals his poorly hidden flowers. "Gracie, I have something for you." Our daughter doesn't move. "It's okay, you don't have to be afraid. It's something nice." He lowers his nose into the flowers. "Something that looks pretty, just like you."

One of the little girls she's playing with puts her hand up. "It's flowers! Can I have one?"

"Not this time," Roger says with a laugh. "These are just for my two girls today."

The kid gives a mocking pout and runs down the slide towards one of the women on the bench.

Roger's smile wanes when Gracie doesn't move. "Don't you want to see what I have for you?"

"I can see what it is. It's flowers."

"That's right, and I have one with your name on it."

"One of the flowers says Gracie?" she asks, confused.

He laughs. "I guess you'll have to find out."

When she doesn't move, I call out to her. "It's okay,

Gracie. Go see your father."

She reluctantly goes down the slide and walks up to him. Roger quickly pulls out one long-stemmed pink rose from the bouquet. The quick motion of his hands seemed to frighten Gracie though, and she takes several steps backwards.

Gracie's cautious look suddenly turns into a smile as she looks behind him. "Ms. Meadows!" she shouts. Annie Meadows is on her bicycle, her long dress flapping as she rides. She slows down a moment and rings her bell several times for Gracie.

"See you tomorrow!" she shouts with a smile as she heads down the road past us.

Roger turns his head back to his daughter. "This is for you," he says, reaching out the rose to her. "It's special because you're special."

Gracie takes it. Roger lowers his head and smells the roses again. "Mm, it smells good."

Gracie does the same and makes the same sound. "Mmm." She laughs. Roger smiles.

"Gracie, can you help me with a special mission?" he asks. She nods repeatedly.

"That's a good girl. Now, take these." He hands her the whole bouquet of flowers. "I need you to help me give these beautiful flowers to the most beautiful mommy here."

Gracie smiles and looks for a moment at the two women across the playground from us. She quickly turns to me and walks awkwardly to me with the flowers in her hand.

"Mommy, these are for you," she says with a huge smile.

I make a shocked face. "For me?"

Roger laughs. "Gracie, tell her why you gave them to her."

"Because Daddy told me to give them to the most beautiful mommy," she says. "That's you."

"Me?" I feign surprise. Gracie nods. "Thank you so much Gracie. Thank you, Daddy."

Roger comes up and pats her head. "Go play for a little more." Gracie runs back into the playground area. I'm a little sad to see the other two moms packing up. I should have asked them for a number or done something. I'm sure if I come back to this playground, they might be here again.

Roger sits beside me on the bench. "Are you okay?" he asks.

"Yeah. You?"

He nods. "Better... now."

CHAPTER 4

Annie

I continue to peddle down the block and think of little Gracie Bradshaw.

She really is a lot like me when I was her age. Mother would have liked to have met her as well.

Thinking of my mother and Gracie makes me sad. I slow down and look back at the child. She's taking a rose from her father's hand and smiling.

"Watch it!" shouts a man in a grey sweater, his hoodie covering his face. "People are walking here!"

"Sorry, sorry," I say with a wide smile. I can't see his full face, except an oddly shaped nose, but know that he hasn't taken my apology well.

I continue to peddle down the street, and a few parents of children I used to watch at the daycare wave at me.

"Hey, Annie!" one mother calls out.

Her little girl, Stephanie, who just started grade school this year, waves frantically at me. "Ms. Meadows!"

"Hey, Stephanie!" I shout back, but not slowing. If I stopped for every child and parent who greeted me, I'd never make it home before sunset. And besides, today I need to visit my mother.

It only takes me ten minutes by bike to get home.

Summertime in Esta is beautiful. It can be baking hot during the day and you need a sweater at night to stay warm. The peaks of the Rocky Mountains surround the town.

It's truly a romantic landscape.

This city may be small, but it's charming. It grows on you. I used to fantasize about leaving it some day when I was a child. The town, and the people who live here as well, including my mother.

I hadn't of course. I found a job as a pre-school teacher at the nearby daycare.

I love my work, and the children love me. Mother would say to me that you never work a day in your life if you love what you do.

That's how I feel every day with the children.

I love surrounding myself with their innocence, their laughter. It makes me almost feel their age, even though I'm nearly twenty-seven now.

In the summertime, I always wear my long summer dresses with different prints on them. Kids, especially Gracie, love them. Her favourite is my yellow dress with bananas on it.

Mother didn't approve of me working with children.

She never hid what she thought and would tell me regularly. She wanted me to be more like her. I never wanted that.

I would rather forget what my mother was.

As I pass the police station, only three blocks away from my home, an officer steps out of the building. Constable Henry Rayton smiles wide at me, takes his hat off and tips it my way.

"Annie Meadows," he says with a joking tone. "Tell your mother I said hello."

"I will, Officer Rayton," I shout back.

I pass the small police headquarters building, and after a few more minutes, arrive home. It's a charming small house in an area known for its older residents. The exterior is painted in a soothing cream hue with a red door. Mother always prided herself on how she cared for her home.

Even though the furniture and décor inside are dated now, she loved how she presented it. Not that we ever had company. That wouldn't work for what she did inside our house.

I pick up my bicycle and carry it up the steps of the wooden front porch.

Once inside, I look around the small living room and the wood panelled walls that enclose me. I go into the kitchen where the cream wallpaper with images of breadbaskets is even less welcoming and open a white cupboard. I grab a glass, turning on the faucet and waiting patiently for the water to cool. I drink a full cup before turning it off. Beside the sink is a door I always keep shut.

It leads to the basement.

I hate going down there now. I try to limit my time there as much as possible. The only reason I need to go down there is for laundry. I drink another cup of water, waiting to find courage to go downstairs and put the clothes I placed in the washer this morning into the dryer.

I breathe in deep, calming my nerves, as I finally do. I walk down the steps slowly, each making a different creaking sound.

I quickly remove the clothes from the washer and put them in the dryer, turning it on. The machine rocks noisily as the drum spins. I must own the loudest dryer in Esta, but it's served its purpose. Sometimes Mother used it to drown out the noise of the people who stayed there. The rooms downstairs were soundproof, but I felt I could still hear them.

I look across the basement at a large bookshelf. Mother and I moved it there to cover the entrance to the other rooms when Mother stopped using those rooms for good. Now my mother's favourite books cover it.

The rooms existed in the home when my family moved in. The former owner was apparently a wine lover. They were his cellars. The owner apparently made his own wine, treading grapes with his bare feet in the smaller room.

I wonder if the former owners had any clue what these rooms would be used for after.

I think of what Mother did in those rooms. What I did.

Someday soon, Mother will die, and the terrible secrets we shared will go with her.

I think of little Gracie Bradshaw again. I can't help it. I've been thinking about this little girl a lot recently. She's quiet. Sad.

She needs someone.

She's just like me. Broken. She needs to be whole again.

A strange beeping sound from the dryer breaks my thoughts, thankfully. The dryer is on its last legs and has started to randomly stop working at times. I quickly turn it back on and head up the stairs, doing my best to not think of Gracie, or my mother.

Never again will those rooms be used. Never again will I let that happen.

I'm not like my mother.

CHAPTER 5
Roger

We sit at the dinner table. Usually, our home is more full of conversation. Today is different, and I know it's my fault.

There's an elephant in the room, and it's me. Gracie picks at her vegetables on the plate and avoids eating more of her taco, which she's only taken one bite out of.

Her eating habits puzzle me. She tends not to eat the most, but when we discover a food she likes, Sarah will try and incorporate it more for dinner time. Nearly two weeks ago, she gobbled up a taco. Sarah's made it several more times since but today she's barely had a bite.

Sarah looks at Gracie's plate and at me. I already know what she's thinking.

"Why doesn't our child eat?"

Usually I would be more demanding of my daughter, but something tells me that raising my voice at this moment will only make things worse. It certainly didn't make things any better yesterday.

"Gracie," Sarah says, looking sternly at her. "You need to eat, hun. Remember what the doctor said to you?"

Gracie flicks a broccoli floret across her plate. "No," she says.

"You need to eat more," Sarah reminds her. "You need

food to grow big and strong, but you won't if you don't eat your food."

"But I'm not hungry," Gracie says, pouting. It's a new thing she does when she doesn't want to do something we've asked. I have to say, it melts my heart every time, but at the moment Sarah is immune to her cuteness.

"Just finish the one taco," she says.

"Can I go play with my toys?"

"Eat your taco and you can."

"C'mon, Gracie," I chime in. "Time to eat, like Mommy says."

Gracie takes a glance at me. For a moment, I see something in her eyes that I recognize all too well.

Fear.

Is Daddy going to yell again if I don't do it?

How do I tell a four-year-old year that I won't? How?

When I was her age, my father would do much more than yell. A belt across my behind would happen as quickly as him attempting to use his words first.

"Okay, Gracie," I say. "How about a few more bites?"

"One?" she asks. I put two fingers up, and it takes her a moment to process what I'm asking. "Okay, two. Two small bites." She smiles at me, and my heart feels better. The fear I noticed in her eyes isn't there now. She's back to smiling at me like normal. I'm no longer the monster from last night.

I remember knowing the monster that my father was. I hated him. I never wanted to be him, and yet yesterday, my little girl looked at me the same way I had my father.

"Roger," Sarah says, "she does need to eat."

I smile. "It's okay, I'll make her a hefty snack before bed."

"Done!" Gracie says, finishing the smallest bites one can make. "Can I play now?"

"Wait," I say. "I need to talk to you first. Yesterday, did Daddy scare you?" Gracie looks at her mother, and back at me, before slowly nodding her head. "I know I did. I'm sorry, Gracie, okay?" She doesn't answer and continues to look at me. "Sometimes, daddies and mommies fight, okay? Sometimes, daddies can go too far."

Sarah clears her throat. "Sometimes moms can go too far as well."

I look at my wife and feel comforted by her words. "Well, yesterday Daddy went too far, and yelled, and scared you and Mommy. I'm sorry, hun. I don't want you to be scared of Daddy though, okay?"

Gracie continues to stare at me, and I wonder what's running through her little brain. Does she smell bullshit?

Sure, Dad. You're sorry until next time you lose your patience.

It was a thought I had growing up; the only difference was my father never apologized.

But I'm not like him.

"You don't have to be scared of Daddy," I repeat. "I promise. Now, go play with your Barbies." Gracie smiles and leaves the table. She runs over to a small toy chest we keep in the living room, takes out several figurines, and immediately starts talking in their make-believe voices.

I breathe out deep while watching my little girl, hating myself for ever making her feel the way I had yesterday.

"She loves you," Sarah reminds me, patting my leg. "I do too."

I nod. "I just... don't know how I lost it like that. I-I'm sorry, Sarah."

She smiles at me. "I accepted the flowers from you. I didn't bash them on the ground or anything. We're okay." She takes her own deep breath. "Did you visit your father today?"

I shake my head. "No," I say. "I thought about going to the cemetery but decided not to. Work was too busy. I had no time."

"Do you want to go together?" she asks.

I'm grateful for her support through this. I used to think losing a parent was the worst imaginable thing.

I knew it was going to happen. It's the logical order of life. First, my grandparents died, and then I got older and had my own child, which means the next to go are my dad and mom.

It was Dad who died first. A massive heart attack while he was watching a basketball game.

Growing up, I imagined what it would be like when my father died. Sometimes I imagined being indifferent. Who cares? The old man is gone. What did he ever do for me?

Other times I imagined me weeping at his coffin.

The reality was much worse. I was every emotion you could imagine. Happy. Sad. Rageful. Or a mix of everything at once.

How do you grieve for someone you never really loved?

That was harsh. I did love my dad, but in a different way than most.

Today, I'm sad. I wish he was still here. I wish we had made up. I wish we were able to connect at least once before he died.

Yesterday I was rageful, and I took it out on my family.

It's been months since he died and I'm still a mess.

"I'm okay," I finally tell her. "Thanks for the offer."

"Well, I'm there for you, Roger. Just tell me, and I'm there."

I nod and smile. "Okay, thanks."

Sarah hasn't lost a parent. She still has both of hers, although she's worried for her father as well. It's been over a year since he had a stroke that took away most of his mobility and speech. He hasn't been able to do much since and is cared for nearly entirely by my mother-in-law.

I thought for sure that he would pass away first, until my father beat him to it.

Finding the courage to look my wife in the eyes, I thank her again. Her eyes are caring and full of love. I wonder what Sarah sees when she looks into mine.

Are they full of anger? Rage? Any semblance of love like hers?

I don't even know who I am anymore.

"Did you see our little girl play with the other children at the playground today?" Sarah says with a smile. She's been so worried about Gracie. I tell her she'll be fine when she starts school. That doesn't stop my wife from being concerned and focused on it. It's the entire reasons she's at daycare, even though we can't afford it.

"I did," I say. "See, I told you not to worry about it."

She nods. "That's what her daycare teacher told me too, but I don't know."

"That's the tall, odd woman with the funny dresses?"

"That's the one," Sarah says with a tone. Whenever Gracie talks about her daycare teacher, Sarah uses the same flat voice when talking about the woman.

Something about her just seems off. She may be a bit

odd and eccentric, but it's evident that Gracie loves being in her classroom. Sometimes I wonder if part of my wife is jealous of another woman having the type of attention Gracie would only give her.

"Hey, I didn't tell you," she says, changing the subject. "I ran into Drew from your work."

"Drew," I repeat, trying not to act surprised. Does she know? Did Drew tell her? "Where did you see Drew at? Did you talk to him?"

She shakes her head. "No, it was at the mall a few days ago when I took Gracie to get some new clothes. He was too far ahead of me. I wasn't able to get his attention. You know his wife, Jenna, was it? I had such a fun time last time we got together. We should invite them over again."

A wave of calmness comes over me. Thank God they didn't talk. That would be the last thing I want. "Yeah, that would be great," I lie. "I'll call him, and we can figure something out." Another lie, of course. Until I tell Sarah the truth, that won't be happening.

Sarah gets up and starts clearing the table. Just as quickly as I felt comforted, a new wave of guilt strikes me.

What am I doing to my family? They're perfect. I'm screwing everything up.

I should tell Sarah the truth about what I'm doing every day. How many lies have I told over the course of a few months now? Soon, I won't be able to hide it.

I look down at my daughter playing with her Barbies and back at my wife cleaning the kitchen. "Hey, how about we go out?" I say.

"What did you have in mind?"

"Well, I think my little girl needs a new toy. A new Barbie? Or a doll, or whatever."

Gracie stands up and jumps enthusiastically. "Yeah!

Let's go!"

Sarah looks at me. "Roger, you said money was tight to me yesterday."

I don't want to remember anything about what I said yesterday. Today I'm a different man. "We're okay," I lie. "Don't worry about the money. Tonight, I want to take my two favourite girls out." Gracie smiles wide at me, and suddenly I feel like the father I was meant to be. "And!" I say, making it more dramatic with a long pause. "After a toy, let's all go get ice cream."

Now both my wife and daughter are looking at me, their happiness etched on their faces, and I feel great again.

CHAPTER 6
Annie

I walk into the Rosewood Medical Center. It's a small building that acts as a hospital for our area. On the third floor is the hospice unit. I continue taking a deep breaths before hitting the elevator button. I often visit my mother, especially now that she doesn't have much time left, but today is different.

I have to see her tonight. The thoughts in my head won't leave.

The elevator door opening shakes my thoughts as I step out and head towards her hallway. A few nurses smile and greet me as I pass them. They've come to know me well since Mother was admitted.

The doctors said Mother was not supposed to live more than a week when she was brought to them. Her ovarian cancer was beyond their capabilities to treat, and it was only a matter of time. The best they could do was give her remaining days as much comfort as she could have.

That was two months ago.

I knew my mother was a fighter. She was capable of understanding what doctors were saying to her at that time, and when she heard she would only have days, she fought to prove them wrong.

Now though, she's getting much worse. I know her time is coming. I've been preparing myself as best I can. Working more. I took up knitting. Anything to keep my mind off what will happen to her next.

Now my thoughts are moving in a different direction though.

Gracie Bradshaw.

I shake the thought of the little girl as I stand outside my mother's room. A nurse steps out of the room and greets me.

"Hello, Melanie," I say. "How is she tonight?"

Melanie is typically a very bubbly young woman. For a brief moment when she greeted me, I saw that side of her personality until I asked her that question.

"She didn't eat today," she answers in a low voice. "Dr. Barry wants to arrange a phone call with you tomorrow as well. Stop by the nurse's desk before you leave, and we can figure out a time he's free."

I look past Melanie at my mother laying in the hospital bed. Her hair is unkempt, instead of styled. Her attire is a dull blue instead of the lively colors she typically wears. Her face has less color as well.

I don't need a nurse to tell me what's happening. I thank her and tell her I'll stop by her desk before leaving.

I take a few steps into Mother's room, feeling it's hard to take more. It's as if some force is wanting to push me out. She's not able to talk to me now. With the heavy medication she's on, I'm not entirely sure she knows I'm here.

I like to think she does.

I kiss her hand. "Hello, Mother." I've grown accustomed to talking to her as if she can answer. I'm not sure how else to act. It seems silly.

She's asleep, or the drugs are in full effect. It's hard to tell most times I visit.

"I ran into Officer Rayton today. He says hi." I smile. "I think he always had a crush on you. I think you liked him too. You liked to talk about him before." Again, Mother doesn't answer and lays in the bed looking lifeless except for an occasional subtle chest movement confirming she's still breathing.

I sit in my chair beside her bed, and take out a book from my large purse. I've nearly finished the entire novel in the past few days during my visits here.

Every so often I peek over at my mother. Sometimes I hope to see her eyes open wide and greet me with joy. That doesn't happen, of course.

I've thought about taking time off to be with her more, but somehow I know she would hate that. If she could, she would tell me to work instead of sitting here with her. That's how she is.

I don't take off time from my job and continue to work and keep my mind busy, even though my heart stays in this room when I leave.

Today's the first day I felt different though.

Today I can't get Gracie out of my mind.

I glance over at my mother again, but she's unmoved from the last glance I had. Lowering my book, I look around the room before staring back at my mother.

I lean in close so that if it's possible for her to actually hear me, only she can make out my words. "The first child you... had, how did you know she was the one? You told me stories, I know, but I was too young to remember that one. How did you know you had to have her? How did you know?" Mother doesn't answer.

A nurse walks by the room but doesn't stop. I clear

my throat and look at Mother again. "I know you said we would never do it again. You told me it was wrong, what you did, but... I can't stop thinking of this child. A little girl. You would like her too." I pause as if my mother can join the conversation.

I let out a breath. "After you stopped taking them, did you ever have the impulse to have another? You told me no, but now that I'm older, I don't believe you... since I have those thoughts."

Mother lays in bed, her breathing labored. Tonight, I had to see her. I thought if I did, the thoughts of Gracie Bradshaw would stop. Looking at my mother would somehow cure me of them.

I only feel stronger urges now.

She's frail and powerless. The cancer will take her soon. I remember months ago when she found out about her diagnosis; she said it was justice from a higher power. She deserved what she had coming for the things she did.

The things I helped her do.

I don't deserve this, though. I close my book and stand up. "I'm not anything like you, Mother." I leave her immediately without looking back.

CHAPTER 7

Sarah

I watch from outside Gracie's bedroom as Roger puts her to sleep. He insisted on putting Gracie to bed tonight. I was walking by the bedroom with a load of laundry ready to put into the washer when I heard giggles coming from her bedroom. I couldn't help but stop and watch the two of them.

I smile as Roger finishes one of Gracie's favourite stories, *The Cat in the Hat*. She loves it when Daddy reads it to her. I have to admit, he has much more expression when he reads compared to me.

Some nights, I just want Gracie to go to bed so I can breathe. It's exhausting at times, and I feel guilty that I just want my own time, or time with Roger. I know I should be in the moment with my daughter more. I'm certain some day I'll look back and wish I had treated this time with her better.

I have a twinge of guilt as I watch Roger and her. They're so happy.

It's a complete 180 from how things were yesterday, and I'm glad about that. I was worried when after Roger was upset, Gracie ran to her room. When I went to her, she was literally shaking with fear.

I didn't know how to react. I just held her tightly until

she calmed. She said he was scared for me. Scared Daddy would hurt her.

Roger has lost his cool, especially lately, but that's one thing he would never do, hurt his little girl. I know that. That's why I'm still with him. If I ever questioned that, I would leave him immediately.

I wouldn't let anything happen to Gracie.

Roger bends down and kisses Gracie on the forehead. "Goodnight," he says playfully. "Love you."

"Goodnight, Daddy," Gracie says with a giggle.

"Sleep tight," Roger says, kissing her one final time on the forehead before turning and seeing me. He smiles, and I do the same.

Roger sneakily crosses the room trying to make as little sound as he can, otherwise the Gracie bomb will go off and we'll have to restart the sleep routine. It's a delicate process. Soon enough she'll be attempting to crawl into our bed and I'll have to put her back to sleep since Roger is usually knocked out.

Roger closes the bedroom door slightly and takes a last glance inside before looking at me.

"What do you feel like doing?" he asks.

"I'm really tired," I say. "I may just go to bed."

Roger looks at me, surprised. "It's not even nine. Are you feeling okay?"

"Yeah, it's just been a long day."

"Well, okay, so- where should, you know, I sleep tonight? I can take the couch again."

I shake my head. "That's okay. I never told you to go to the couch to begin with. You did that."

He nods with a thin smile. "Well, it didn't feel right sharing a bed with you after… I feel better today though; I hope you do too."

"I do," I lie. I tell myself everything in my marriage is perfect. I tell myself I'm happy. I tell myself that the things that are bad will change.

I tell myself Roger will change.

Sometimes I wonder how stupid I am. Then again, I have a beautiful daughter. A husband who supports us. What else can a woman ask for?

"I think I'll just read in bed," I say.

"Me too," Roger says, and he follows me to our bedroom.

Eventually, as we lay in bed, I start hearing the sounds of Roger falling asleep. It starts off as strong gushes of breath coming from his mouth, followed by louder snores.

When I'm certain he's asleep, I turn over and watch my husband.

Roger is a complicated man.

When I first met him, I was taken by how cheerful he seemed. He was always smiling and cracking jokes. He was so much fun to be around. Now that we've been together for over a decade, I've seen the other side of him. The parts he hides well.

The anger.

Before going to bed last night, I brought it up again, much to his dismay.

Therapy.

Couples therapy. It's something I've mentioned before. Roger wasn't very open to the idea.

I never thought I'd be a woman who felt they needed therapy to get along with their husband. What has happened to my marriage?

Roger lost his father. That's a big part of it. Things weren't great before his father died either, though, if I'm being honest.

When you're completely stuck on what to do in a marriage that's not going well, I asked for what I thought the cliche answer was. Let's talk to someone.

Roger said no, though.

I went to see my doctor. She prescribed me anti-depression pills. I still have the prescription in my purse.

Maybe I'm just as stubborn as Roger because I haven't filled it yet. I haven't taken a pill, and if I'm being honest, I don't want to.

I just need my marriage to be better, and I don't need the pills.

Tonight, in bed, I brought up the idea of therapy again, and to my surprise, Roger agreed.

"Okay," he said. "You book it. I'll be there."

When I watched Roger put Gracie to sleep, I worried I was too stupid to realize that Roger will never change. Tonight proved that he can. He's willing to give therapy a try.

As I continue to watch my husband drool from the side of his mouth and snore louder, I just hope, pray, that things will be better.

I know Roger loves me. He adores Gracie. He would do anything for her. Will he change for me?

CHAPTER 8

Annie

What do I do with this house after my mother passes? It's been a thought I've had ever since she moved into the hospice.

This place has terrible memories though. I hate it.

I stare into the dark room where Mother used to keep the children she took. One of the four walls is painted white, with a blue sky above. A yellow sun with a smiley face is in the middle. I remember the day my mother painted it.

It was my idea. I thought the children were sad and having a mural would help them.

As much as I like to think it was all my mother's doing, I participated. I helped her.

I imagine burning this house down to the ground. I would love nothing better than to see it, and all the memories that go with it, turned to ashes.

Would that help me move on from what she did?

I think of Gracie Bradshaw again.

"I'm not you," I say to the empty room. I look at the smiling sunshine and, out of character, curse at it. "I'm not my damn mother!" I close the door.

What Mother did was wrong. I may have thought differently when I was a child, but I know better now that

I'm older.

As I got older, I realized I was too young to understand what was happening. Mother told me we were helping them, after all. I know she lied now.

She may be sick and dying, but she was ill before her cancer diagnosis. She was what many would consider to be a monster.

And I'm her daughter.

What does that make me?

I lean against the heavy door. The exterior is wood but underneath it's steel. Nearly impossible to break. It locks from the outside, and Mother even installed brackets to put a two-by-four on to reinforce the door should anyone try to break free.

I can almost hear the muffled shouts of those who were inside these rooms even now. I pound on the door out of frustration. The sound triggers a memory of a young boy on the other side once, hammering on the door for his parents. I wanted to unlock the door immediately, but Mother wouldn't let me.

"He doesn't understand," Mother had told me when she saw the tears rolling down my face. Billy Hopkins was his name. I remember all of their names.

Mother wouldn't allow me to let Billy go that day. She continued to lie to me and say we were helping them.

I know that's a lie.

Mother is a liar. What we did was wrong. When I was eighteen, I started a journal and wrote all my memories of each child locked in this room that I could remember. If I had any courage, I would walk a few blocks down from my house to the police station and turn it in for evidence.

I would give the book to Officer Rayton himself so he could stop romanticising what he thought my mother was like and see, for once, what I lived with my entire life.

What would the police do with me? The answer was obvious. I was my mother's unwilling accomplice.

I wasn't so unwilling when I was just a stupid child myself though. I happily helped Mother with what she did, thinking it helped.

Eventually, I started including past newspaper clippings of the children taken in my journal too. I documented everything I could.

Mother said she stopped when I turned sixteen. Sure, she didn't keep any more children in our basement, but how did I know she didn't do other things outside of this house?

Children continued to go missing. How do I know my mother didn't have a hand in that as well?

As much as I love her, I'm ready for her to die. Is that sad to think about? She's my mother, but she's also a monster.

I'm not like her.

I would never do the things she did. Never.

I slowly walk up the stairs to the main floor of my home. I'm stuck in this house forever. I can never sell it. If I do, it's just a matter of time before the world finds out what we did in this basement.

Perhaps the only thing I can do is set it ablaze. If I ever have the guts to do it, I should set fire to this house and stay inside it, watching it be destroyed as well as ultimately myself. Poetic justice for what's happened here.

I sit at my kitchen table and think of making myself tea. The warm drink always calms me when I work myself up, which is often.

On the table is an array of pictures the children at the

daycare made for me the past few days. Sometimes when I drink my tea, I look at them to remind myself who I really am.

A good person.

I'm not my mother. Not anything at all like her. I actually want to help children. I pour water in the kettle and turn on the stove, looking at the pictures on the table as I wait.

I pick up one that has a few scribbles on it. On the bottom is the letter M. Matthew gave it to me yesterday and said it was a gift. He said the lines were somehow a ghost. I'm not sure how one could make out a ghost from the image he made, but I thanked him for the gift nonetheless.

I get a lot of gifts from the children. They love me. They do.

I look at some other pictures made for me. Lana made me a decent looking picture of a sunflower, with a stick figure with missing legs beside it. She said that this was me smelling the beautiful flower. She was no doubt inspired by the dress I wore that had different flower heads on it. I love dressing the way I do at work. It makes the children so happy.

The kettle begins to boil, and a slight hissing sound comes from the spout.

I take a deep breath as I pick up the picture Gracie made for me today. Her gift was different from the others.

It was special.

She needs me.

She doesn't know it, but she does. Just like I didn't know it when I needed Mother's help.

My mother is dying now. She isn't around now to do anything. She can't save a child like Gracie now.

It's just me.

Can the terrible things our parents do be passed to their children through their genes? Am I the same monster my mother was?

I look at Gracie's gift and know I'm not anything like my mother. I would never take it as far as she did.

I don't have to be like my mother, but Gracie needs me.

She needs to be pure again.

CHAPTER 9
Sarah

I'm already running super late today. I was late getting myself ready. Late dropping Gracie off at daycare. I was so desperate for time that I nearly unbuckled her seatbelt and opened the door for her to jump out of the car and go in by herself. When Gracie seemed a little lost on what I wanted her to do, I had to remind myself how young she is and walked her inside the building.

Annie Meadows was waiting for me inside. She had that strange smile she always had plastered on her face as Gracie ran up to her. The two held hands as Annie brought her into the room where the rest of the children were. Even though I was late, I watched the two of them for a moment. There was something about the way they went down the short hallway together that bothered me.

Gracie didn't even say bye to me before leaving with Annie. After realizing I was gawking and standing in the daycare alone, I was reminded how late I was.

This morning I have an important meeting with my former boss. Gracie had been a surprise pregnancy for Roger and me. I had only started working at JJ Insurance a month before I found out. I didn't qualify for maternity leave, so I wasn't guaranteed my job when I wanted to come back.

After having Gracie, though, Roger and I decided I would stay home a few years until she started daycare.

Sometimes I hate myself for that decision. My child would have likely benefited from the social interaction earlier. Now she was that loner kid who kept to herself in the group.

I was the same. When I see her, I can't help but think of myself when I was younger.

It took me years to find some friends. Now I'm in my thirties and have no friends at all. How am I supposed to help my daughter with her social skills when I have none myself?

Now that Gracie is in daycare though, things will be better. She'll make friends, eventually, just as I did.

So will I, once I return to work. Today's meeting is to discuss me coming back to JJ Insurance. I'm surprised that my old boss would even bother seeing me. It's been years since I worked there.

I had supposed that was a good sign. The actual meeting is even better.

I get my old job back. I can start in two months. My former, now again, boss, says this will be the next training session for new hires, and she wants me to start fresh again. A lot of things have changed since I left and she wants me to be set up for success.

I feel high with happiness. The years of being a stay-at-home mom were nice, but a lot of it was lonely and it felt like I only had Roger in my life.

Now, my days will be full of conversations with actual adults. Not that I didn't love talking to my little girl, but I'm ready for lunch dates and coffee outings with work friends again.

It feels like a new chapter of my life.

After the meeting, I decide to visit my parents. I want to tell Mom the good news. Besides Roger, my mom has been the only other source of adult conversation over the past few years. She would tell me otherwise, but I know that she was a little upset when I told her I would be going back to work and that Gracie was starting daycare.

Mom wanted Gracie to stay at her home during the day. I thanked her for the offer but told her it was important for Gracie to get used to having more children around her. Besides, Mom had Dad to care for now.

Since his stroke nearly two years ago, he's been a shell of the scary man he used to be. The stroke took away his mobility and speech. Mom has to take care of him completely now. Not that it's much different to before. She did everything for the man, but you wouldn't know it the way he spoke to her.

When things weren't done a particular way, which was to his liking, you would hear it. Now you hear nothing. Mom usually places him by the window during the day, or near the television watching sports.

I'm not sure if he's truly watching it, though, besides the occasional grunt he makes.

It's sad to say, but visiting my parents has become a lot easier to bear now that he can't say a word.

One time I suggested to my mom that maybe he should stay at a nursing home. She refused. She said she was still able to care for him. She didn't work. They had enough money to live comfortably. The least she could do is tend to her husband's needs.

Maybe I've become too resentful for living with that man for as long as I did, but I don't know if I could. He may not be able to speak now, but for decades he did, and most of what he said was not nice.

I shake my negative thoughts and think about how happy I'll be when I'm back at work. Gracie has only been in daycare for one month, I only brought up working again with Roger a few weeks ago, and I already have a job!

I was worried about passing out resumes when I have several years of unemployment. I'm sure I would have eventually found something, but I assumed it was going to take a long time.

The meeting with my old boss makes me feel like I'm on a cloud. I didn't exactly love the job itself, which is funny to think about as well. In fact, I quite disliked it. Maybe it's being around people again that has me happy.

Before visiting Mom, I stopped by the grocery store to pick up a few things for dinner tonight. I can't wait to tell Roger about my day.

I feel like my mind has been in a fog for some time. Depression, my doctor calls it. I was given a prescription to remedy it. Now that I'm going back to work, I feel like I don't need meds. I just need to feel like my old self again. Gracie is getting older, and I can go back to being who I was a little more.

As I'm passing the bread aisle, I spot Heather, Roger's coworker. I remember not liking her so much. She's a pretty young woman who worked reception for Roger's company. At a Christmas party one year, I thought she had a few too many drinks and I didn't like how I spotted Roger and her talking privately by the bar. She laughed a little too easily at Roger's jokes. That was years ago, though, I remind myself.

It is weird seeing her at a grocery store at this time. Shouldn't she be at her desk at Roger's company? When Heather spots me she smiles and waves. She walks up to me, nearly banging her cart into mine.

"Sarah, hey," she says with her wide smile.

"Heather, how have you been?"

"Good. How's Roger doing?"

I try not to get annoyed that she asked about my husband immediately. Why is she even asking? She sees him nearly every day. "Fine, good." I smile. "Surprised to see you around here, though. You have the day off or something?"

"Well, I quit a few weeks ago, actually. I started school for nursing."

"That's wonderful," I say. Wonderful that you won't be seeing Roger anytime soon again as well.

"By the way," she says, her expression becoming something more serious, "I'm so sorry to hear about what happened with Roger. Please tell him I think what they did to him wasn't fair."

My own pretend smile vanishes from my face now. "What do you mean?"

Heather shakes her head. "The way they fired him was wrong. It shouldn't have happened. You know his boss, though. After the years he put in there, they should have given him a second chance."

I collect myself, trying to refrain from shaking Heather into telling me everything she knows. Roger isn't working? He's been fired? What happened? I have so many questions and I don't know where to start.

"Right," I say in agreement.

"I can't believe it's been three months since they fired him," she says. "I'm glad I left too. Tell Roger I said hi, though."

I most certainly will not. I'll be too busy asking him why he's been lying to me.

CHAPTER 10

Annie

It's been a typical day for anyone who can't read what's happening in my mind. A normal routine for those who attend or work at a daycare. First we did crafts. Afterwards, I entertained the children with my 'magic tricks' I call it.

The kids find my double-jointed fingers fascinating. I'll move my thumbs in awkward positions and hide them behind me. When I reveal my hands again, the fingers are back to their normal position, I'll shout out 'magic' and the kids laugh and clap, especially Gracie. Now they demand I do my magic everyday.

For a moving activity, I got the children to follow me in a conga line. Gracie was immediately behind me. I try to involve her more in group activities to encourage her to play with others.

It doesn't generally work out, though. As soon as the activity is done, she goes back to playing by herself. Just like I did when I was her age.

I was alone too for most of my young life. Mother didn't want me to play with others. She said it was too dangerous. Now that I'm older, I know why she prevented me.

She didn't want me to say the wrong thing.

How easy it would have been for me to slip and tell others about what happened in the basement, especially when I was young. Mother normalized it so much that I assumed everyone had people in their basement. Why would it be weird? Why would it be wrong? Mother said we helped them, after all.

And I believed every word.

From across the room, I tell two young boys not to hit each other over them wanting the same toy. A conversation I've had multiple times.

When the boys agree to not fight any longer, they both move onto different toys within minutes and forget entirely about the one they fought about.

Typical.

It's so easy for children to forget.

When they become older though, some will remember what happened when they were younger. I did. The children in the basement will.

I take a deep breath and walk over to the office area, letting my partner know I'll be right back.

I quickly glance at Gracie, playing alone with her dolls in the corner of the room before I leave.

"Stop, stop. I don't have to do anything," I tell myself. "Let it go."

I walk over to the bulletin board. Lately the daycare center has been testing having weekend hours. It's been successful. Many parents seem to enjoy having day dates or just a morning to themselves to decompress from work and the demands they have as parents throughout the week.

I'm happy to take on that demand. Besides, it's overtime, and I need to stay busy. I need to keep my thoughts at bay. The impulses I have need to stop.

I sign up for some hours this weekend, and for a change, I actually look at the bulletin board at work. One section in particular has my attention. A group of pictures of men who are known child predators living in the city. The police provide us with updates of people we need to watch out for.

From time to time, I look at the pictures of these men. Most don't appear harmful. Some are quite normal looking. You could pass them in the street without knowing they belong on a list of terrible people who have done terrible things.

I take my time looking at one man's picture. A white man in his mid- thirties. Jeremy Timmons. The only thing that makes him different to anyone else is a crooked nose.

People pass me every day, and none know what I've seen. What I've done. If they knew, my mother's face would join the group of men on this board.

Mine as well.

I stare at the board and notice my supervisor, Mabel, looking at me from her office chair. I let her know I signed up for some extra hours on the weekend. She thanks me for the help, and I head back to my room, where my children are playing.

Only one of them looks up when I come in.

Gracie.

I smile, walk over and sit beside her. "Can I play with you?" I ask, and her small face lights up with a smile.

CHAPTER 11

Sarah

I knock on my mom's front door, and she opens it with a wide smile. We hug briefly before I come inside.

"Hey, Sarah," she says. "I was worried you weren't coming."

I'd rather be here than my own home right now. The idea of facing Roger is nauseating.

For months, my husband has been lying to me. How many more lies has he told without me knowing?

What has he been doing during the day? Where does he go? I've been home the entire time. Why couldn't he tell me? I could have helped him.

Mom and I embrace again, and as we enter her living room, I see my father facing the window, looking out into the front yard. He doesn't greet me, of course. He can't now. He wouldn't have even if he was capable, though. Before the stroke, he would have, at most, perhaps raised a hand in gesture that he understands my presence is around him as he continued to watch his sports.

Another thing I'm glad about Roger is that he hates watching sports. Although right now my husband isn't my favourite person.

"Say hi to your dad," Mom reminds me.

Mom's been good at encouraging me to speak to him.

It's hard to understand that under the shell I see in front of the window, my dad is still alive and understands what's happening on some level.

I walk up beside his wheelchair, reach for his hand placed in his lap, and grab it. "Hey, Dad."

I look outside at the view he has. My parents live on one of the older streets in town. It was constructed during a time when the builders cared about aesthetics. Large trees line the road. Through the branches I can see the peaks of the Rockies.

It isn't a bad view, but I can't imagine looking at it for hours on end.

"How's he doing?" I ask Mom, letting go of his hand.

"Well, you know, no changes. But the other day he made a sound I hadn't heard before. I told the doctor. I thought it sounded like a word. He says there's still a chance that his speech can return."

I look at my dad for a moment. His speech was the worst part about him before the stroke. Seeing him now, he's like a stray dog that can't bark anymore.

Mom's in the kitchen, and I already know what she's doing.

"I'm not hungry, Mom," I say. "I'm okay."

"You sure?" Mom says to me with a smile. I again tell her and she starts whistling a tune while tidying up. It's hard to know what the song is from her terrible whistling, but it makes me smile. I don't remember her looking so happy before. Part of me thinks she enjoys taking care of Dad like this.

Mom's whistling stops. "And where is my beautiful granddaughter?"

I walk into the kitchen and sit at the small table there. "At daycare, Mom. You know that."

"Right," she says with a tone. I wait for her to tell me again that Gracie can stay with her if I need a break at home. That paying for daycare isn't needed. For a change, she doesn't. She continues whistling as she tidies some things she left out from making lunch.

From the moment I came to see Mom, I wanted to tell her about Roger. After learning about his lies, at first I wasn't planning on coming here; I was too upset. But then I realized I have no one else to talk to about it.

"I've got good news," I say, focusing on the nice stuff instead. "I got my old job back."

Mom turns to me. "Really? That customer service job at that insurance company?"

I nod my head. "I had a meeting with my old boss today. I was so happy to find out she still worked there. We chatted for fifteen minutes over coffee, and she hired me on the spot."

"Wow! That's great news. They must be desperate to hire people."

I sigh. Not exactly the words I wanted to hear. My old company must be in a bad spot to hire someone they haven't seen in years? Gee, thanks Mom.

"Well, my boss, Linda, always liked me. I start in a few weeks. I'm excited to go back to work."

"Really?" Mom says again with surprise. "You always hated that job."

I sigh again. My mom never worked. Dad wouldn't let her. Somehow they managed to raise a child and have a small house on one income. That wasn't possible anymore. Besides, how do you explain to a woman who has never worked that even though you complain about your job, you secretly like going sometimes?

"How's your arm doing?" she asks.

I move my shoulder in a small circle. "The physio helped. I had an ultrasound the other day, and the doctor says it's all better. I can go back to lifting a hundred pounds over my head again." Mom smiles at my joke.

"That's good dear. Want tea?"

I shake my head, but Mom puts the kettle on for herself.

For a moment, I think about telling her about how the doctor also prescribed me pills for depression. How do I explain to a woman that dealt with my father for decades without medication that I need something to help?

I'm just as stubborn, though. Sometimes I think about what my doctor said to me during our last appointment. Part of me thinks about filling the prescription at the pharmacy. The majority of my mind is against it. I wonder if that's because I compare my life against my mom's. If she didn't need meds to get by, why do I?

I glance over to the living room, at Dad staring blankly outside the window, and back at Mom. "Did Dad ever get angry to the point you were actually scared of him?"

Mom looked at me with concern. "Did something happen with you and Roger?"

"A bad fight. That's all. He threw a dish. It came close to hitting Gracie." Mom's mouth gapes open. Before she could say another word, I try to alleviate her worry. "He didn't try and hit her. She was just in his path."

"Why was he so angry?"

I still don't fully understand. We were talking about Gracie at daycare. I was worried about how she wasn't talking to other children. I was worried that it was my fault that she was that way. We have a small rec center in town with a pool. I should have taken her there more, instead of my mom's house. I should have tried to go to more local events where I could have met other moms. Arrange playdates. Do things where she could have met other children. Instead, I did a lot of nothing.

Roger thought maybe Gracie could go to part-time daycare since I wasn't working. I reminded him that I was going to look for a job.

As I continued to talk about how much I hated myself for not giving Gracie more opportunities to play with other children, Roger started to agree with me.

"Yeah, why didn't you do more?" He would add other comments. Kicking me when I was already down. I shouted at him. I shouldn't have. He took his plate and the remnants of food on it and whipped it across the room. Gracie, who must have heard her name several times in our heated exchange, came into the room and was nearly struck.

She cried for a long time after that in fear. Roger immediately snapped out of his rage and attempted to tend to her, but Gracie only wanted me.

None of this I would tell my mom.

"It was nothing," I lie. I've been lying to myself a lot lately. None of it I wanted to tell my mom, though. "It's not worth getting into. We talked it through, Roger and me. He wants to do therapy with me."

"Therapy?" Mom says with a laugh. "Wow, times have changed." She pauses for a moment. "I mean, that's good, dear, really it is. I hope you two work out whatever's happening." She laughs again. "If I ever tried to get your dad to do therapy, well, I don't even know what he would say. He wouldn't say yes, that's for sure."

That's certainly true.

The kettle starts to whistle, and Mom turns off the stove. "You two make a good team, though. Roger's a good man. I'm sure you guys will work this out."

I sigh one last time. A good man who's been lying to me for months.

CHAPTER 12

Roger

I step inside the daycare pickup area and ask for my daughter. After a few moments, Gracie comes out of a room and stares at me. She looks around and steps back inside the room.

I take in a deep breath. I thought we got over what happened. I thought after yesterday, and how we got along after she bought a few Barbies, that everything was forgiven.

Water under the bridge.

Right away, from the look she gave me, I knew I was wrong. I truly scared my little girl when she was nearly struck by the plate I threw.

I had no clue she was even there. I hadn't meant to hit her. I didn't see her. It was a mistake. After I heard the plate smash into pieces, and Gracie weep, I immediately stood up and tried to make things right.

There was no consoling her though. She only wanted Sarah. Only her mother could make things better. What did I expect? Daddy had become a monster that night, so of course Mom was all she had in that moment.

Still, when Sarah asked me to pick up Gracie today, I thought things would be different. I should have told her that I couldn't. I wouldn't usually be able to. When I was working, I would never have been able to leave early to get Gracie at this time.

Of course, I have no job. I've been unemployed for months. Sarah doesn't know that, though. I should have lied to her about not being able to pick up Gracie. Why not add another lie to the pile? What's one more?

Before coming here, a small part of me feared this. I remembered how well last night went when I put her to bed. I thought we were going to do much better together.

When Sarah asked if I could pick her up, I thought this would be a great time to make things even better.

The moment my daughter saw me without her mother, she ran away. I don't blame my little girl.

Gracie comes back out of the room, this time with the daycare worker Annie Meadows with her. She's attempting poorly to hide behind Annie's flowing white dress with little police cars on it.

"Gracie, it's Dad," I say. "I'm here to pick you up. Are you ready to go?"

She doesn't answer and instead peeks around Annie's dress, hiding behind a police car once again after looking into my eyes.

I'm trying my best not to make a scene. The last thing I want is for Gracie to tell everyone what happened. The last thing I want to do is explain why my four-year-old is scared of her father.

"Sarah didn't mention you were picking Gracie up today," Annie says. Something about her tone upsets me. I know I'm not usually the one to do it, but I'm not exactly a stranger.

"Sorry," I say instead. "Sarah's at her mom's for a late dinner. She asked me to pick her up. I wasn't aware that we needed to inform you guys."

"It's just policy," she says again. "Next time, please let us know if there are any changes. You understand, of course."

I'm nearly grinding my teeth. Of course, I understand there are terrible people out there who would do terrible things to children. I'm not one of them. I think of the plate smashing and my daughter's tears.

I'm not one of them, I remind myself.

"I understand," I say. I go around Annie and kneel in front of my daughter. "Gracie," I say, in the softest voice I can manage, "Mom is with Grandma right now. She asked me to pick you up. I wanted to spend some Daddy time with you. Is that okay?"

Gracie is doing her best to not look me in the eyes. My own are starting to water. I quickly rub the tears away.

My own daughter, scared of me. What have I done?

I stand up and look at Annie. "Sarah and I had a bad fight," I say in an even lower voice that I spoke to Gracie with. "I think Gracie is just scared. You know how marriages are." I laugh.

"I'm single," Annie says in a deadpan voice. She kneels to my daughter now. "Okay, sweet pea, Daddy's here. Are you okay to go home? Mommy is going to be home soon too."

As if she said something different than me, Gracie nods her head slowly. Annie hugs my daughter before Gracie stands beside me.

"Thanks," I say, amazed at the turnaround in her.

"Have a good day, Mr. Bradshaw."

I take Gracie's hand, and we go out to the car. As we do, she's giving me the silent treatment. She seems to have learned that well from her mom. I imagine the rest of my life I'll have two women who will be doing this to me.

I take in a deep breath. Gracie must be the only little girl at the daycare who doesn't want to go home. What does that say about me?

There's a way to make things better again. Time and trust. I automatically had trust being her father. That's temporarily broken now. I just need to get it back.

I imagine my daughter, decades from now, sitting in a psychologist's room, telling the doctor how terrible I was. I have my own stories too. My father was much worse. Had it been him, he would have been aiming at me for target practice with multiple plates.

Unlike Gracie, I have actual scars to prove it.

I think of the hatred I have for the man who created me. I never wanted my own daughter to have similar feelings for me,

I stop walking and kneel to my daughter's level again. "I scared you, didn't I?" I ask her. She doesn't answer me. I don't blame her again. "Daddy didn't mean to hurt you that night. I didn't want to hurt anyone. Daddy is just an angry person, and sometimes I get too upset. I do bad things that I'm very sad about later. Daddy can be a dumb guy. Like a big poo head." For a moment Gracie smiles, and my heart feels lighter. "An ultimate poo Head," I say, upping the level of crap.

"Mommy says you're just sad," Gracie says in a soft voice. I take a deep breath before she continues. "Sad, about Grandpa."

I nod my head slowly. "That's right. That doesn't make it okay, though, but Daddy is very sad about Grandpa."

"Are you sad that he's in heaven?" she asks innocently.

I take another deep breath. If only she knew what my father had done to me, she would know he is nowhere near that place. "Yes," I lie. "I'm sad that he's in heaven." After a moment of silence, and my knees shaking, I stand up. "Mommy's with Grandma right now, and she won't be home for dinner. How about I take you for McDonalds?" I say in a fun voice. "Chocolate sundae after!"

"Oh, yes!" Gracie says with enthusiasm. "'And, Daddy, can we get another Barbie?"

I laugh. Is my daughter now extorting me?

"We'll talk about it more after we eat. Okay, let's go, sweet pea." I open the car door, and Gracie jumps in.

As I buckle her in her car seat, I wonder why I called her "sweet pea". It's something I never say to her. Maybe part of me is jealous that Annie Meadows seems to have a better connection with my own daughter than me. Maybe I want my daughter to see me more like her.

I'd settle for her not looking at me as if I'm the monster.

CHAPTER 13

Annie

I decided not to visit my mother today after work. Unlike yesterday when I felt the urge to see her, today I'd have done anything to be as far away as possible. I didn't want to look at her. Despite not wanting to think of her, I'm in bed with my journal firmly in my hands.

I've been lying here for what feels like forever, frozen in time. I've wanted to open my journal, but something almost supernatural has been keeping me from doing so.

Finally, I manage to open the first page. It's an old picture I took from a camera my mother bought me when I was young. Mom took a photo of both of us, after she did our hair in pigtails. We're both smiling. It's such a beautiful picture, but too bad no one understands what happens after the photo was taken. The reality of what living in this house with my mother was actually like.

I do though.

The next few pages remind me exactly what she did. Newspaper headlines are stapled to them.

"Borden family still missing. Foul play suspected."

"Family asks for help in finding a mother and her son who's still missing."

I stop on a page reading another headline. "Body of missing person found." I quickly turn the page. That was one I didn't want to read.

I remember what happened the day my mother read that article herself. I was much older at that point. It was close to when Mother said she would stop. She was worried she would be caught. She didn't, though. She lied. She continued. Not even the fear of the authorities finding the decomposed body of what she had done would stop her.

Then I go to the last newspaper page of my journal. This was the last one she took. I was nearly sixteen at the time. I read the headline and look at the picture of the missing boy. He was only three years old. He could barely understand what was happening. A handsome young boy with light brown eyes, who was so full of life.

Even when he was locked in our basement, by himself, he barely cried.

I spent a lot of time with him. I think of us reading books underneath the yellow smiling sun. We read a lot of books. He stayed many nights with us.

Mother eventually did stop. She refused to tell me why.

Thankfully, that was the end of everything.

Now it's different. It's as if the impulses Mother had with children have been passed along to me.

I'm not my mother, I remind myself.

Then why can't I stop thinking about Gracie Bradshaw? Why can't I stop thinking about me reading with her under the smiling sun in my basement?

I imagine me tearing another newspaper clipping and adding it to my journal, only this time it's for something I did.

I can no longer blame Mother for what she's done if I do the same.

Mother would never have picked Gracie. Never choose a child you know personally. That's how you get caught.

It was a rule. One of many Mother had. Before she stopped, she attempted to train me in her ways. Little did she know I never intended to use them, until I met Gracie.

I think of her and how she plays alone. She's just like me at her age. I think of Sarah Bradshaw. She seems like many other mothers. She's more interested in herself, and not her child. She doesn't care what has happened to her daughter. She doesn't care that she's broken.

I do.

Never choose a child you know.

It's as if I can hear my mother's words coming straight from her mouth.

It's impossible, of course. She can barely manage to say anything now.

I lower the journal in my hand.

"Break the rules, and you get caught," I say out loud.

CHAPTER 14

Sarah

I finish drying and putting away the dishes, every so often glancing at my husband, who's lying on the couch, looking at his phone.

I can hear Gracie playing with her toys in the other room. I hear new make-believe voices coming from her and can tell she's playing with the Barbies that Roger bought her. She also came home with some dinky toys from her happy meal.

Roger laughs to himself, staring at his phone, as I place the last dish in the cupboard. I wonder why the man can't help me with more chores, seeing that he literally does nothing all day.

Is he even looking for work? Several months is a long time to be unemployed. Roger handles all the finances for our house. Apparently it isn't too hard to hide his inactivity.

Despite that, how could I not know that he hasn't been working?

Had I known, I would have given him a broom and asked him to help around our home for a change. I usually do more of the cleaning and cooking, seeing that my husband "works all day".

I haven't told him I know that he's been lying. I

haven't really said much to him since coming home from Mom's. I stayed for dinner. The last place I wanted to be was my own home. I was worried about what I would say. I was worried we would fight again.

Before closing the upper cabinet, I look at the pile of dishes neatly stacked inside. The last thing I want is for Roger and me to fight like we did several days ago.

I know I need to say something to him. I just don't know how to approach it in a way I feel good about.

Am I scared of my own husband? Have I come to a point where I'm nervous to say something to him out of fear of how he'll react?

I never thought I would end up like this.

Roger agreed to therapy. From what I know, therapy is all about communication. We're going to have more opportunities to figure out how to talk to each other better. I know that.

So what if I don't say anything to him right now about me knowing he's not working? I just need more help on how to talk to my husband again.

Roger laughs again, watching some stand-up comedy clip on his phone. His laughter irritates me. What could be so funny?

Part of me wants to storm up to him, grab his phone and smash it in front of him. Suddenly that feeling of fear I've had for him vanishes.

I sit on the couch opposite him.

"I didn't tell you about my meeting with my old boss," I say.

"Right, how did it go?" Roger doesn't turn off his phone or even lower it from his face. That irritates me even more.

"I got my old job back," I say with a thin smile. At least

one of us will be employed.

He lowers his phone. "Really? That's great."

I wonder how much longer we could have gone without Roger working before we lost our house or the power went out. Roger told me we had some money saved up for an emergency fund. How much more would be left in that account before he told me? Now that I'm going to start working again, how much more will he extend his vacation from work?

"I start in in a few weeks," I say.

He makes a sour face. "Why so long?"

Why is he making that face? I wonder. Is it because we have no money left? Do we need the money from a job now to make ends meet? He's been buying Barbies and McDonalds for Gracie even though we have food in the fridge and our daughter has plenty of toys.

"They have training starting soon. My boss wants me to be retrained since it's been some time since I was there. A lot has changed in the past few years."

A lot has changed in my own home too.

"I see," Roger says. "I wonder if you could start earlier though?"

"Why?" I ask innocently. "Are we doing okay?"

Roger nods rapidly. "Yeah, I just know you wanted to go back to work. Besides, daycare is expensive."

I remember when I started at JJ Insurance, years ago, Roger hated it. He didn't want me to work. He said he could provide for me and our family. I stupidly listened to him. I don't regret my time off work with Gracie, even though I do regret not doing more with my daughter.

"How was your day at work?" I ask him, waiting patiently for his response.

"Good." I wait for him to say more, but he doesn't. He

won't come clean now. He hasn't for months. Why would he finally start now? What else is he lying about?

"Thanks for picking up Gracie today," I say. "It must have been tough to get time off to do it."

Roger almost appears to frown, and for a moment, I feel he's going to tell me the truth. "Well, yeah, I had to talk to my boss, and he didn't like it, but I told him it's my daughter. He has kids, so he gets it."

I want to stand up and dig my index finger into his chest, telling him I know the truth. I want to give it to him, like he does to me whenever we fight. You can almost see steam coming from his head when he's angry.

I glance to the kitchen table, where the last fight we had occurred. Where he raised his voice, scared me to death, and broke the plate, nearly hitting our child.

It was a mistake, he claimed. How many mistakes has my husband made? How much more should I take? I never thought I'd be a woman to take half of what I had with my husband.

I need him though.

I think of the sound the plate made when it smashed against the wall. The sound of Gracie crying. My fear that she'd been hit or was bleeding.

I stand up, but instead of confronting him, I do the more reasonable thing: pretend I don't know.

Roger goes back to his phone and his laughter.

I go back to doing more chores.

Perhaps it's better this way.

CHAPTER 15

Sarah

I leave early to get Gracie to daycare. It was a nearly impossible task to get a young child to ready for the day, but with some gentle rushing, I succeeded. I dressed her in a red dress and tied her messy hair with a matching ribbon.

I have a mission in mind, and that involves getting her to preschool as soon as I can.

When I arrive, Annie Meadows has a wide smile on her face. There's something off-putting about the way she smiles, and she's always doing it. She looks like a maniac with how happy she must be.

Whenever I see her smile, it unsettles me. It's her eyes. No matter how happy it makes her seem, her eyes are unchanged. They would almost fit better on a person on the verge of crying or about to explode with anger.

I ignore my thoughts and give my own smile back. "I'm a little early today. Hope that's okay."

"No problem," she answers. She comes closer to my daughter and grabs her hand. "Good morning, Gracie."

"Morning, Ms. Meadows!" my daughter says with enthusiasm. She looks at the young woman's dress. Today she has a ladybug pattern on it. I somehow know that Annie must sew them on these dresses. At least I hope she does. I can only imagine the horrific store she buys all these clothes in otherwise.

"Oh! I love ladybugs," Gracie says. "Mom, can I wear a dress like Ms. Meadows? Can you buy me this one?"

I laugh. "We'll talk about that later, but Mommy has to go." I wave at Annie and thank her again before leaving. I suddenly remember I forgot to give my little girl a kiss. I turn quickly and kiss her forehead. "Love you."

"Mom!" she says, annoyed. "You got your spit on my head."

I quickly rub her forehead with my hand. Annie just continues to watch us, that smile of hers getting wider.

"Thanks again," I say to her.

"Sarah," she says quickly. I turn to her, thinking I don't have much time left.

"Yes?"

"Will you be picking up Gracie today, or your husband?"

"Umm..." My mind is whirling with where I need to be, and I'm struggling with the easy answer. "Me, as usual," I finally say.

Her smile vanishes for a moment and returns soon after, even larger and more unsettling. "Wonderful. Have a beautiful day." She grabs Gracie's hand again, and I watch them for a moment as they walk into the classroom.

My mind immediately goes back to my plan, and I near jog to my car in the parking lot. Instead of my usual Starbucks run, I go straight home. I don't take the usual streets. I circle around to avoid them until I'm coming up my block from the opposite way I usually take.

I smile when I see Roger's car still parked in the driveway.

He knows I take my time coming home after dropping off Gracie. He must have thought he had a lot more time to diddle around the home before leaving and diddling around somewhere else.

Today, I'm going to get answers. What has my husband been up to these past few months?

What other secrets has he been keeping?

I would love nothing more than to park at my house and confront him about why he's still home. Maybe he would actually tell the truth for a change.

I was too nervous to tell him I knew the truth when I realized I don't, not really. I don't know what he's doing during the day.

I park over a block away from my home and patiently wait. I see a figure exit and suddenly Roger's car is leaving the driveway. I start my car but don't move. All it would take for my plan to be thwarted is for him to drive past me. Thankfully he doesn't. When I see his car go the opposite way, I put my car in drive and begin to follow.

I've never tailed someone before. It's not the life I lead, but it's funny the skills you find in yourself when you need them. Apparently I'm good at following people without arousing suspicion, staying far enough away but not too far to keep track of where he's going. Instead of getting my old job back, I laugh thinking I could have become a private investigator.

Roger makes an unexpected right turn from the furthest lane away. I quickly merge into the other lane and follow him down a side street. Did he spot me while I was daydreaming?

I look down the street but can't find his red car anywhere. I bang on my steering wheel until I spot it in the parking lot across the street. I pull into the entrance and park on the other side. I wait a few moments to ensure he's not getting out of his car, then step out and look at the building.

Esta Public Library.

What would Roger be doing here? Maybe he found his true calling as a librarian. We can both take new career paths together. Me a PI and him, his nose in a book in a library.

Somehow I know that's not the case, though. I step into the building, knowing this is another time it would be easy for my husband to spot me.

I don't exactly have an excuse as to why I would be here, but neither does he. I feel safer with other people around too. He'd be less likely to fly off the handle in public. I feel ashamed even thinking this, though, about my husband.

I look around the large building. I feel ashamed that I never stepped inside the local library as well. To my right there's a long staircase to the second floor. Roger could be anywhere.

"Can I help you?" an older woman behind a desk asks me.

"No, I'm okay," I tell her. "Just browsing." I turn my head looking for my husband but don't spot him.

"What genre?"

"I'm sorry?"

She laughs. "Books. What genre of books are you looking for?"

I shrug. "So many good ones," I say. "If I need help, I'll come back, though, thanks." She smiles and nods.

I begin to search the place. I start in the back, trying to conceal myself behind bookshelves in case I do spot him. I look up, thinking I should go upstairs to see if I can spot him, when I notice a computer area.

Sitting at one of the stations is Roger. He's typing away at the keyboard and looking intently at the screen.

I quickly hide behind a bookshelf and peer at him.

"True crime," a woman's voice says. I turn and the elderly librarian from before is smiling at me. "I didn't take you for a true crime reader."

I take a book off the shelf. I peer at the title. *The Night I Killed my Wife*. I quickly put it back. "Well, I'm still shopping around," I say. I roll my eyes thinking how stupid I sound. "Thanks again."

When the woman leaves, I sneakily go around the bookshelves until I can see Roger's back. I need to see what he's doing on the computer. A younger man, who could even be a teenager, is sitting a row before Roger, playing some game. I can only imagine Roger doing the same. I'm not sure if I could keep my cool if he was.

I get closer, trying to not draw attention to myself, ready to hide behind a bookshelf with the slightest motion from Roger. When I'm close enough, I see what he's searching for and suddenly feel very foolish.

Job postings.

He's clicking on different searches, looking and reading each post. I let out a breath and wondered why I thought he would be doing anything else.

How many days has he been coming here to look for work? How many unsuccessful interviews has he had too?

Roger reaches above his head, and I quickly jump behind a bookshelf. I see him pat his mouth as he yawns.

"Romance now," a familiar voice says. I turn and the librarian is laughing now as she wheels her cart and puts some books on a shelf. I continue down the aisle and try and to ignore the woman, who seems to be everywhere.

I continue to watch Roger for some time, while also avoiding the librarian. At some point it's going to be obvious that I'm not here for books. Roger continues to seemingly look for jobs. I'm nearly about to give up, when he stands up from his workstation and gathers his things.

I watch him as he leaves. I follow at a far enough distance.

Where is he going now? My suspicions won't allow me to go home and forget about everything. I need to know what my husband is doing. Is it as innocent as looking for jobs while not telling me?

Has he been too proud of a man to tell me he's not working but looking for work?

When I trail him out of the building, the librarian is at her station near the entrance. "Have a good day," she tells me. I give a thin smile back and wave goodbye. I can only imagine what the woman may be thinking of me but get my mind back on following my husband.

I scurry to my car and again begin following him.

What I find out this time is earth shattering.

He stopped at a cafe. Alone. Sitting outside on a patio enjoying his drink. I watch him from my car and continue to wait for a random woman, perhaps even Heather, to suddenly sit with him.

Of course, that doesn't happen.

I begin to feel even more foolish for the anger I've had at my husband since finding out, until what he does immediately after the coffee shop.

This time I follow him down familiar roads. We're just outside our small city. With dread, I suddenly know where he's going, but need to see it for myself.

When he drives past the arches of the entrance to the

cemetery, my heart sinks.

He's visiting his father.

I was so obsessed over what my husband has been up to during the day, that I'm suddenly struck with guilt over finding out the truth. He's been looking for a job and visiting his deceased father.

I wipe a tear from my eye and stop my car just outside the cemetery gate.

No more following Roger. I'm giving up my job as a PI forever now.

When he comes home, I'll be waiting for him. No more lies. The anger I had for him is gone. When he tells me he's been at work all day, I'll tell him about the conversation with Heather.

No more lies.

CHAPTER 16

Sarah

I've never paced around my house this much. I can't concentrate. At the beginning of today, I wanted nothing more than to scream at my husband for lying.

Now I feel nothing but sadness for him.

The rational side of me knows he won't be back soon. He needs to continue the lie. He doesn't know that the jig is up. Why would he suddenly come home early?

He won't, but that doesn't stop me from pacing, attempting to stay busy while also trying to think about how to handle the conversation I need to have with Roger.

I want him to feel supported. No matter what happens with his job, he needs to remember that we're a team in this. I still need to know what happened, though.

There's no time to wait for a psychologist to help us learn to communicate better. I need to talk to my husband now. I was worried about how he would react, but that was before when I was angry and confrontational. Now, I'm feeling more supportive.

Seeing his car drive into the cemetery hit me hard. I almost wanted to follow him inside, but this time to reveal my presence. I imagined myself standing beside him while he stood near his father's gravestone and holding his hand.

I didn't do that. Instead, I went home and tried my best to stay busy while watching daytime television. So much drama in the shows I watch during the day, but for a change I have more in my real life.

When Roger does come home, we'll talk about everything. I'll just tell him the truth. I'll tell him how I found out. I'll ask him what happened, and I won't get upset.

I won't get upset, I remind myself.

Roger may get triggered when we talk but I won't do the same. I'll be calm and supportive. I'll remind him about the vows we took the day we got married. My husband hasn't been himself for some time.

I know that it's time I show it.

I won't get upset, I remind myself a third time.

I look at the stove clock and realize how long it's been. Somehow time speeds up when you don't want it to.

The thought suddenly strikes me that I need to collect Gracie; I'm more than late this time. They charge per minute over and the last thing we need right now is to pay extra for daycare.

I quickly grab my purse and head out the door. I try my best to get to the daycare before pick-up, but it's hopeless. Living in a small city won't help me today. I'm nearly twenty minutes late. My mind drifts as I drive frantically in traffic on how my talk will go with Roger.

There's a good chance he'll be home when I get back. I dread it. I just want it to go well. I don't want us to fight. I don't want Roger to lose his cool. I don't want any more accidents to happen. The last thing Gracie needs to see is her father angry again.

I park in the lot and head inside. I'm greeted by the center's supervisor for a change. Mabel's eyebrows arch when she sees me.

"I know, I'm late," I say. "I'm so sorry. If you charge me that's okay. It's just been a day."

Mabel nods back. "Okay. I thought Gracie left already."

I look at her, surprised. "What do you mean?"

"There's just one little boy whose parents we're waiting for. I was pretty sure Gracie left."

I take a deep breath. I take out my cell but don't see a message from Roger. He never picks her up. Yesterday was a one-off situation.

"So Roger picked her up?" I ask her.

Her mouth gapes open a moment. "He must have."

I dial his number and impatiently wait for my husband to answer. "You don't know if my husband picked up my daughter?" I ask Mabel, slightly annoyed.

"No, sorry. Usually Ms. Meadows handles pick-up. I'm afraid she left for the day already."

When Roger doesn't answer1 I hang up and look at Mabel. "Well, where is she?"

I follow her down the hallway. A small boy is sitting on a bench picking his nose.

"James," Mabel says, "do not leave this bench until you see your mom, okay?" The small boy nods, and digs his finger in deeper.

We walk into the empty classroom. I search around and even open a closet door.

"I don't understand," I say. I try to calm myself. "I mean, she must be with my husband then, right?"

Mabel nods. "I'm sure. Ms. Meadows is pretty good with parent pick-up and drop-off. She's very strict with our rules."

I remember the conversation I had with her this morning when she asked who would be collecting Gracie.

I remember her odd smile when I told her it would be me.

"Can you call Annie?" I ask her. "Sorry, I mean, Ms. Meadows."

Mabel's mouth gapes open again. "Of course. Let me go to the office and do that."

The little boy from the hallway comes into the room. "My mom's here!"

Mabel looks at me. "Let me take care of this quickly and then call Ms. Meadows, okay?"

I nod in appreciation while trying to calm myself. When the supervisor leaves the room my phone buzzes in my hand. I'm relieved when I see Roger's name on the display.

I answer the call immediately. "Hey," I say to my husband. "Is Gracie with you?

CHAPTER 17

Roger

"No," I say. "Was I supposed to collect her?"

"The daycare says you picked her up today," Sarah says, her voice strained.

"No," I say again. "I've been at work all day. I just got off. I'm driving home now. I never went to the daycare."

"She's not here," Sarah says frantically.

"What do you mean?"

"Gracie isn't here! Gracie is not at the daycare. They thought you picked her up."

"I'm on my way," I say. I turn my car around. Sarah keeps me on the phone as I hear her talk to another woman.

"My husband doesn't have her," she says.

"Ms. Meadows says when she left, Gracie was still here," the woman says. "Maybe she's still here?"

"Who is that?" I ask, starting to feel anger boil inside me.

"Mabel," Sarah says. "The supervisor at the daycare. She wants to look around in the other rooms."

We end our call, and I speed even faster until I finally arrive. I push the daycare door, but it's locked. I bang on the windows until an older woman opens it for me.

"Did you find her?' I ask immediately. "Is she here?"

Sarah comes down the hallway slowly, tears falling. "She's not here, Roger."

"What? How can this happen?" I look at the supervisor, my rageful eyes demanding answers. The older woman looks like she could shrivel up and die in front of us.

Thankfully, the door opens again and in walks Annie Meadows.

"Oh, thank God you're here," Sarah says.

Mabel talks first. "We can't find Gracie in the building. Are you sure you didn't see her leave before you left?"

Annie looks at me and my wife. Her usual perky and odd aura has disappeared. "She was still here when I left."

"I don't understand," Sarah shouts. "You people have a whole process for picking up and dropping off kids. Annie, you told me that just this morning. How could she have left without anybody knowing?"

Annie looks at my wife, her mouth shut as if she has no words to explain what happened. Finally, she manages to find some, looking at her boss. "When I told you I was leaving, I let you know there were still children, remember."

"Right," Mabel says. "You mentioned Gracie and the other boy."

"So, what happened after that?" I demand.

"There was a phone call in the back office," Mabel says. "I only left for a moment."

"Right," Annie says. "That's when I left. But I saw your car, Mr. Bradshaw. Usually, the kids know not to leave without us present. She must have done though."

"What the hell are you talking about?" I say. "I wasn't here."

"I'm going to go look at the playground," Sarah says.

"She could still be outside." She nearly barrels me over as she leaves.

I look at the old lady and Ms. Meadows in disbelief. "Where's my daughter?"

My worst nightmare is confirmed as Annie answers the question honestly. "We don't know."

CHAPTER 18

Sarah

Roger and I speak with officers together and separately. We sit on the benches where the little boy was an hour ago, waiting for his mother to pick him up. It should have been where Gracie was too.

My little girl is now missing, and nobody has a clue where she could be.

The police are looking over video surveillance of the property, trying to figure out where she could have gone. They tell us what they've discovered.

Nothing.

Video shows Gracie in the room all day and outside during play time. When they watched pick-up times, they didn't see her leave. At some point, she didn't show up on camera. No footage showed her exit.

The police interview Annie Meadows as well. She stays the entire time, sitting on a bench across the hall. Every so often she looks up at us but quickly looks away.

Rightly so. I could kill her. My little girl is gone, and this freak lost her. Had she not left and properly watched my child until I picked her up, none of this would happen.

She had to leave early, she reported. Her supervisor took over and did a really crap job of watching the children.

Annie says she thought she saw Roger's car in the parking lot. Police are still looking at multiple camera angles to figure out what happened while we wait, impatiently.

Roger looks at Annie, unable to close his mouth. "Why the hell did you leave work early? You couldn't have watched our child until we came? No, you had to just leave. What could be so important?"

Annie takes a deep breath. "My mom's in hospice and is about to die."

Roger's cold eyes lighten a moment, and he lowers his head. "This is pointless," he says, saying what I'm only thinking. "We need to go look for her. No more talking to the police. That gets us nowhere. We've been here for over an hour."

"She wasn't at the park," I say. I looked there and around the area until police showed up. I stayed in the park, hoping that any moment I would see my little girl come down the slide laughing.

She didn't. She hasn't been found. She's still missing. This hell continues.

"Mr. Bradshaw?" a woman in a grey suit asks. She has a gold police shield chained around her neck. "Mrs. Bradshaw?" She doesn't wait for us to respond. We're obviously not entirely here right now. "I'm Detective Falls." She puts out her hand, but my husband doesn't shake it.

I do.

"Do you have any more information?" I ask.

"Not right now. I've been assigned to your daughter's case. I'm here to do everything we can to find her, but I need your help."

"What do you need?" Roger finally says.

"A most recent picture of what she looks like to start. I'm going to talk to my superior about putting out an Amber Alert immediately. We want to circulate as much information as we can about Grace today."

"Gracie," Roger corrects her. He lowers his head.

I take out my cell phone and provide her with the details of the red dress she wore to daycare today. The red hair ribbon she wore. Detective Falls asks me to email several pictures. I'm amazed to find I have one with the red dress as well. I send her nearly a dozen. It takes a lot of willpower to not look at my sweet little girl's face as I scroll through my photos to find ones that I think will help the search.

Deep breaths, I remind myself.

The detective takes out a notepad. "Now, I know you guys spoke with the police already, but I just wanted to go over a few details again. Sarah," she says, looking at me. "You were going to pick up Gracie today, but Annie —" She now turns to the teacher. "—you say you saw Mr. Bradshaw's vehicle in the parking lot."

She nods. "I was sure I saw it before I left. I had to go for personal reasons."

I take a moment when Annie says those words.

"I wasn't here today!" Roger shouts in frustration. "That wasn't my car! It wasn't me."

Annie is visibly shaking at my husband's aggression. The detective looks at the young woman and asks her to step into her classroom as we continue to talk. When she's out of the hallway, Detective Falls looks at my husband. "And where were you today, Mr. Bradshaw?"

He sighs heavily. "At work, all day." I stare at my husband and his brazen lies. Why is he willing to lie to a detective even now? "I don't usually pick up my daughter from daycare."

"But you did yesterday," Falls says.

"That's right. It was just the one time. It was my first time picking her up from here ever, to be honest."

"Okay, and what about—"

My husband cuts off the detective and stands up. "I've had enough of this, really. My daughter is missing, and my wife and I are here, answering your questions, helping you guys fill out paperwork, but none of that will help my little girl. We're leaving," he says, looking at me. I stare at him coldly, and when I don't move, he breathes out. "Fine, I'm leaving. I'm going around the neighborhood. Someone must have seen my girl."

Detective Falls turns to him and tries her best to use a sympathetic voice. "I understand. This isn't my first missing child case, and it won't be my last. I've already dispatched officers to help. We have others looking at tape. This is a top priority right now, I assure you. It's best if you stay here while we figure out timelines and understand what happened today."

Roger points at the classroom where Annie is. "That stupid woman lost my child. She 'didn't pay attention. And that other stupid woman," he says, pointing towards the supervisor's office where Mabel is showing the officers the video, "is just as bad. They're responsible for this. Where could she have gone? She's only four! She didn't leave with someone else, it seems, so she must have gotten out of the daycare. She has to be outside somewhere. Maybe she got lost. I don't know."

"You think she ran away?" the detective asks, brushing her blond hair to one side. "Is there a reason why she would want to?"

Roger strikes the wall of the daycare's hallway,

leaving a mess in the plaster. "I'm leaving. I'm looking for my girl. Sarah can help you. I need to actually do something about this." He storms out and starts wandering down the street.

The detective turns to me. "I have a difficult question for you, Mrs. Bradshaw. My officers say that during one of your interviews with them, you mentioned that you and your husband were fighting recently. Did Gracie see this fight?"

I breathe out. "Yes, she did."

"Was there a situation of domestic abuse, or anything like that?"

I lower my head and my mouth gapes open. I feel frozen. How much should I say?

When I don't answer, Falls continues. "And Annie Meadows mentioned that she saw your husband's car before she left. He says he was at work, but is there any reason you could think of that that may not be true? Is there any reason why your husband would have picked up your daughter without telling you?"

I look up at the detective. "My husband is a complicated man, but he would never do anything to hurt Gracie." I think of my daughter crying after he nearly struck her with the plate. I think of our fights. I think of everything all at once, making it hard to breathe or think clearly.

I shake my head. "But my husband is lying to you. He's been lying to me for some time."

CHAPTER 19

Annie

Detective Falls walks into my classroom. She looks around at some of the children's artwork on the walls, focusing on one where the kids glued pasta together to try and make something resembling a person.

"Were any of these made by Grace Bradshaw?" she asks.

I tighten my bottom lip and look around. I finally manage to spot one of hers. "That one," I say. Different colored stick figures with no arms and a bunch of circles.

I don't tell her about the gifts Gracie made me before. The ones I keep at home. That would ruin everything.

"How are you doing?" she asks me.

"Okay. Gracie is a very special child. I hope we figure out what happened soon, and she's found safe. I don't blame the Bradshaws for being mad at me. It is my fault."

Detective Falls looks at me with her own tight bottom lip now. "How's your mom?" she asks. "Some of us at the station have been meaning to visit her. You probably don't remember me that well, but I remember you when you were a teenager and your mother would bring you to the Christmas parties at the station."

"I remember fondly," I say, and it's true. Cassie Falls was an interesting woman. In a world of mostly male detectives, she stood alone at her station as the highest paid woman on staff. My mother said that she could be chief someday, if she wanted the job. Somehow I knew differently. She loved what she did, just as my mother had.

Mother wouldn't admit it, but someone like Cassie Falls scared her. She was the type of woman who could put the pieces together. Discover what Mother had done. She hadn't thought.

That doesn't mean I can take her lightly.

"Mom is... not well," I finally answer. "She's in the hospice unit now. She doesn't have long."

"I heard that," she says. "I'm sorry. You know, your mom was the best report processor we ever had at our station. People still talk about her. We were so upset when she decided to retire early. Lot of officers had to do better work on their reporting after she left because nobody else could pick up the slack of what she did for everyone, including me."

"That's nice of you to say." I flatten my dress and sit on a chair. "I suppose you're going to want to talk to me more."

"I know the other officers already spoke to you, Annie. I just asked you to come inside this room to cool off Mr. Bradshaw. He seems to get a little red. I understand, and I'm sure you do, but he had me worried. What's he like?"

"I don't know him well," I answer truthfully. "He picked up Gracie yesterday. I think that may have been the second time I've met him. The first time was when he came with his wife to tour the daycare together."

"Are you sure you saw his car today before you left?"

I take a moment before answering. "That's what I

thought. He drives a red Toyota Camry, though. Not uncommon. I could have been mistaken. I'm not really thinking straight. I'm sorry."

Cassie nods. "Right. I know you have a lot on your mind. You wanted to leave early to visit your mom, was what I was told."

"Like I said, she doesn't have much longer."

"Okay, well, I think we got everything we need from you. If you think of anything else, just let me know." She hands me a card with her name and number on it. "Call anytime if you think of anything. The first few days of these cases are important."

I nod, and when Detective Falls starts to leave the room, I call out to her. She turns to me and waits for me to speak. I question if I should mention it, until it feels right to say something. "There was something strange that happened yesterday. Mr. Bradshaw came to pick up Gracie, and she was scared of him. It was like she didn't want to leave the daycare." I laugh. "The poor thing was tied to my hip."

"Did she say why she was scared?"

"Mr. Bradshaw said that he and his wife got into an argument the other day and it must have scared Gracie."

Cassie nods. "Thanks for the info."

I lower my head. "I just hope Gracie's found soon. Please tell me when you find anything. I can't believe this happened." Tears begin forming in my eyes, and I allow them to freely drop down my face. "This is all my fault."

Cassie puts a hand in her jacket pocket and pulls out a handkerchief. She hands it to me, and I wipe my face. "This isn't your fault. Whoever has Gracie Bradshaw, that's who's fault this is. That is, if someone took her. We still don't know anything. It's hard to believe she just walked away from the daycare on her own without being noticed."

More tears roll down my face.

Detective Falls looks at me with concern. "Annie, everyone knows how great you and your mom are. Don't worry. In the end, this won't come back on you. I'll tell you when we find her, okay?"

I nod and pat my cheeks, unable to keep them dry. I attempt to hand back her handkerchief, but Cassie waves me off. She tells me to take it easy on myself before leaving my classroom and the building. From my window, I watch her as she gets into her unmarked police car.

Suddenly my face goes back to its neutral expression. My eyes stop tearing and I pat my face dry as I stoically watch Detective Falls drive away.

CHAPTER 20

Sarah

We drive around the neighborhood that surrounds the daycare, every so often stepping out of the car to look around and call out for Gracie. It's nearly pitch dark out now. I know we're starting to get on people's nerves, and at one point someone opened their window to yell at us to shut up. Roger yelled back a four-letter word starting with an F followed by "you". Thankfully, that person closed their window before anything escalated.

The last thing we need is for Roger to end up in jail. I need his help. We need to work together to find our little girl.

We run into a constable who's also interviewing neighbors and business owners, conducting his own investigation. Roger nods and thanks him for the help. The constable walks towards a convenience store and Roger lets him know that he already spoke with the owner and even checked the footage of the camera outside.

The constable thanks Roger and heads off.

It's been several hours since anyone has seen our daughter. If I wasn't so focused on finding someone who has, I'd be curled up in a ball crying.

"Maybe we should call it a night," Roger says. "It's

been hours, and we've gotten nowhere. We can wake up early, print off pictures of her. Put them around town. I don't know."

"I'm staying out here," I say. "I'm not letting my little girl freeze outside tonight. Not. Going. To. Happen."

Roger lowers his head. "She's not out here."

"And how do you know?"

He shrugs. "I don't, not really. But we looked everywhere."

"I'm going to check the alleys again."

"We've been down there so many times."

"You're already giving up? Today in the daycare, I thought you cared about finding our daughter. Now, when it's not going the way we want, you to leave. What, you're scared? You don't think I'm not? We must find her."

He turns away from me for a moment, then looks back, his eyes full of anger. "Why did you show up late? You couldn't have come early for a change?"

"Come early!"

"I've had a few bills from the daycare already that show how late you are sometimes."

"Right," I say. "It's too bad you were at 'work' and couldn't have picked up Gracie yourself. Or apparently, you did."

"What the hell are you talking about? I never picked her up today. I was not here. I was at—"

"Work!" I cut him off. "Yes, the job you were canned from months ago! Right? That one?"

Roger is speechless. "How long have you known?"

"Yesterday," I say truthfully. "I ran into that floozy, Heather, and she told me everything. How many days have you lied to me?"

Roger stands beside the car and looks into the empty

street. "Gracie! Where are you?" His screams have a slight echo and sadden me as he tries again to somehow conjure up our missing daughter by saying her name three times.

It's not going to be that easy.

"You've been lying to me!" I tell my husband.

"I was trying to find work. I was—"

"I don't care about that right now. I just want to find Gracie!"

"And I don't?" He looks down at his phone. "Detective Falls texted me. She wants to meet at the house. She has more questions."

"More like questions for you, Roger."

"What do you mean?"

"I told her about your lies. I can't believe our daughter is missing and you're lying to a detective about where you've been all day. Why? Just so I wouldn't find out? You think I wouldn't have found out?"

He sighs. "Okay, so you know. The detective knows. That doesn't change anything. We still need to figure out what happened."

"I know!" I shout and point down the road. "That's why I'm going back into the alleys."

Roger raises his phone. "The detective. We should go and talk to her."

"You can do that," I say. "I'm staying right here until I find her. I'll call a taxi to get home." I start walking toward the alley and can tell Roger is watching me. "Just leave!" I shout.

I hear the sounds of the car door opening and closing and the ignition starting. I turn my head once just to watch my deceitful husband go.

It's not his fault, but I can't stop thinking that had I not been following my husband around all day, because of his lies, I would have been at the daycare to pick up Gracie on time. None of this would have happened.

If he never lied to me, our daughter would be with me right now, and I wouldn't be walking around an alley by myself at night.

Esta isn't very large and not known for its crimes, but typically I would never be here like this by myself at nighttime. As I pass the back of a bar, two men are smoking a cigarette. One of them blows out smoke and hollers at me to come over and talk to him.

I ignore him.

I put my hand in my purse and grab a set of house keys, putting the largest between my index and middle fingers. If anybody tries to approach me tonight, I won't be so patient. I need to find my daughter.

In the dimly lit alleyway, it's getting harder and harder to see anything. I take out my phone and put on the flashlight trying to see what I can. I call out my daughter's name several times but hear nothing in return, besides the laughter of one of the two men outside the back of the bar behind me.

I look at my phone and realize with fear that I have less than fifteen percent battery left. It's been nearly thirty minutes since Roger left, and I'm still wandering aimlessly through alleys, finding no signs of life except drunkards.

I realize Roger was right. I should get some sleep, if that's even possible. We can come up with some kind of plan on what to do.

As my phone illuminates part of the dark alley, I spot something in a pile of trash. When I realize what it is, I quickly open the garbage bags around it and throw everything round.

My daughter isn't here. I pick up the red ribbon I used to tie her hair this morning. My daughter isn't here now, but at some point she was.

CHAPTER 21

Roger

When I park in my driveway, Detective Falls is already waiting for me on the front porch.

"Anything new?" I ask immediately.

"Is Sarah coming?"

I shake my head. "Just me."

"No big updates, but let's talk more inside."

I unlock the front door and welcome her in. She sits on the couch and gestures for me to do so, which I find odd as it's my living room.

"I think we need to talk, Mr. Bradshaw," she says. When I sit, I look at her, confused. "This isn't going to go well for either of us if you're not telling the truth."

I nod. "Right, I wasn't at work today."

"Why didn't you tell me that?" she asks, tilting her head.

I sigh. I'm tired of these accusations. "I didn't do anything bad here, okay. You people are looking at me like I'm somehow involved in this. You need to stop this and go out and find out who has my daughter!"

"That's what we're doing. But your lying makes our investigation more difficult." She opens her notebook. "You need to be honest, and we're not off to a good start. Not only were you not at work, but you haven't been employed since—" She scans her notebook. "—June. That's a long time to not tell anybody, but then I see from your record why. Assault. When were you planning to tell your wife that you attacked your former boss?" When I don't answer, she continues, "Were you waiting for the trial?"

I lower my head. "I've been stressed."

She closes her book. "Your father passed, I understand." I nod. "Things have been tense at home with Sarah. Your daughter too."

I reluctantly nod again. "Yeah," I answer. Short and sweet, but for a change the truth.

"Sarah told me about the plate incident too."

I breath out. "Not a proud moment. I'm not winning father of the year, I know that. Where are you going with this? I lied in the moment. I realize I shouldn't, and I won't anymore."

"Have there ever been any more situations of abuse in your home?" she asks, getting to the point. "Any reason why Gracie would want to run away?"

"You think she ran away? Sarah and I, and half a dozen cops, have been looking around all night. Someone would have found her if she ran."

"Has there been any other issue in your house we need to know about?"

I sigh. "No. The plate scared Gracie. Scared her a lot. Do you really think she ran away from home because of that?"

"We're still considering all options but not ruling out kidnapping."

"I see. Well, you've made your point. No more lies. I'm an open book. Whatever you need from me, let me know." Even though I'm being honest, I say my words with a hint of a tone. I don't know why.

She nods. "I was hoping Sarah would be here for this as well, but I have a folder of some pictures I'd like you to look at."

I nod back, and she grabs the folder beside her on the couch and places several pictures of men on the table in front of me.

"Do you recognize any of these people?"

I look at them. Most of them are rough looking except one man in a grey sweater with a button shirt underneath.

"I don't think so," I say. "Who are they?"

"Known offenders in the area that target children."

I cover my mouth and look at the faces again. There's a least a dozen pictures on the table. I never thought Esta would have so many pieces of shit living here.

"All of these men are from town?"

She shakes her head. "No, they're just the ones close enough to the daycare. Many times, we find that with predators, they tend to scout."

"Scout?"

Detective Falls stiffens her bottom lip. "They plan ahead. They watch children while they make plans. I just wanted to make sure you never saw any of them before. It's likely nothing, but it's worth having you look just in case. My officers are planning on speaking with all of them anyway."

I take a handful of pictures and examine each individually. One manages to catch my attention above the others. Jeremy Timmons. It's specifically his facial figures that I remember. I turn the picture to the detective.

"I think I've seen this man," I say. "The other day I met

up with Sarah and Gracie at the playground across from the daycare. Before we left, I saw a man sitting on a bench. I don't remember much about him, besides him being alone. I didn't see any children near him. I remember the oddly shaped nose though. Do you think this man was involved with Gracie?"

The detective looks at the picture and makes a note in her pad. "I don't know, Mr. Bradshaw, but we're going to find out. I'll leave these pictures for Sarah to look at."

"Where does that man live exactly? How close to the daycare?"

"I'm going to speak to him personally, so don't worry, okay."

"I'm going to worry!" I shout back. "If he has my daughter, you need to investigate this immediately!" I lower my head and try to calm my nerves. "Some monster has Gracie. Who knows what they're doing with her."

CHAPTER 22

Annie

I lift the large kitchen knife, inspecting the blade. I brush my finger against the edge, feeling its sharpness.

Or lack of sharpness.

The blade is dull, and it's time for a new one.

I plunge the knife into a bunch of celery, cutting it into small pieces, and adding it to a plate. I grab baby carrots from the fridge to join the growing collection of vegetables. In the middle is a pile of ranch sauce. I put the plate and tall glass of water on a tray.

This brings back memories.

It's something I did many times over, bringing food to children in the basement. Only usually it was Mother who prepared it.

Now it's just me doing everything.

As I head towards the basement, I think of how smoothly everything went today. I've also thought of the many lies I've told.

Mother hated telling lies herself, but it was necessary.

I take my time heading down the stairs and I lose my footing, spilling some of the drink into the vegetables on the plate. I suppose I'm not so smooth now.

I lied when I said I wanted to leave early to visit my mother.

I instructed Gracie on how to exit the daycare. I know where the cameras are. I've looked through the feed before. When Mabel is away or sick, sometimes I act as the supervisor.

I told Gracie we were going to play a special game.

Gracie did well following my instructions. She waited patiently to see me after I left through the front door.

The game was simple.

Hide in the alley across the street until Ms. Meadows finds me.

When I did, Gracie laughed but I put a finger to my lips, reminding her that we had to be very quiet, as I had instructed earlier.

Gracie's very good at following instructions. She listened well. She did as she was told. She followed me to my house, at a distance. I took a special way home, avoiding the police station entirely.

At this point we played another special game. Follow Ms. Meadows without her catching you. Gracie followed me as I quickly walked towards my house. Every so often I'd look back and Gracie would attempt, poorly, to hide.

It was risky, of course. Something Mother wouldn't have approved of, but I made it home with Gracie not far behind. She came inside and followed me to the basement. Now she waits for me as I bring her snack.

I told myself if someone saw me, and reported it, that what I was doing was wrong, and I would accept my fate. It's been hours though, and the police haven't shown up at my front door.

What I had done was- right. Gracie was meant to be with me.

I try wiping the water from the vegetables as I go past the bookshelf that I've pushed aside. I stand outside the locked door of room one. I place the tray on a nightstand and remove the length of timber that bars it from the outside. I knock on the door before entering, since I still have manners.

I smile as I open the door and the little girl has an infectious smile that I have to match. I carefully place the tray on the table inside beside the door and close it behind me.

Gracie gets off from the couch, where I've been reading to her for hours. She sits at the table, and I join her.

"I'm sorry I had to leave, sweet pea. I brought you a night snack," I tell her. "After this, you can change into some pajamas, and it will be time for night night."

Gracie grabs a carrot and dips it in the ranch, making a yummy sound as she chews. "Um, I don't have pajamas here."

I smile. "Don't be silly, of course you didn't bring any. This was a last-minute sleepover. I bought you some. There is a dresser next to the bed."

Gracie looks around the dimly lit room. "Ms. Meadows, I'm a little scared to sleep here. That sun scares me." She points at the yellow sun with a wide smile in the blue sky.

I smirk. She isn't the first child to say something similar. "That's okay, sweet pea," I tell her. "I'll stay here as long as you need me."

Gracie grabs a piece of celery now. "Why do you have to keep shutting the door?" she asks, nearly inaudible from the food in her mouth.

"Finish chewing before you ask a question, Gracie," I remind her. "Remember how I tell you this at daycare."

"Yeah," she says in a mocking voice.

"Well, I lock the door for your safety. I don't want anything bad to happen to you, so I lock the door."

"Am I going to daycare tomorrow?" she asks.

I shake my head. "We're having a special sleepover," I remind her. "Just the two of us! We're going to have such a great time. And!" I say enthusiastically. "I have a present for you."

"Present?"

"Close your eyes, sweet pea." Gracie does as asked. I go to the dresser beside her bed and take out the special dress I made for her. I bring it to her and ask her to open her eyes.

"Ladybugs!" Gracie shouts. "A dress with ladybugs like yours."

I laugh. "Now we can match. I'll wear my bug dress tomorrow."

"Thanks, Ms. Meadows."

I poke her nose. "My pleasure, sweet pea." She laughs.

Gracie's smile disappears a moment. "When can I see my mommy?"

It's a question that's been asked so many times to me in this room. Every time it hurts my heart to lie. "Soon, sweet pea, soon. Well, eat up, it's getting late."

"Can we watch another movie?"

I shake my head. "No, that was a special movie time because I had to leave for a little bit. Now, finish up your food and I'll read you a goodnight story too."

Gracie raises four fingers. "Three books, okay?" she asks.

I laugh. "I'll even read four, sweet pea."

"Can I have a chocolatey snack? My mom always gives me one before bed when I've been good."

I shake my head. "You have been a good girl today, but

as my mother used to say, sugar rots your teeth and your mind."

CHAPTER 23

Sarah

Within minutes of me calling the police, multiple cruisers arrive on the scene. The responding officer asks me to show him exactly where I found my daughter's hair ribbon. I do so and describe how I found it. He immediately asks me to leave the area so that a forensic team can look more into everything.

More police officers arrive, and soon, so does Detective Falls. She greets me and I explain again how I found the ribbon.

"We need to search around here for my daughter!" I plead.

Falls nods. "That's right, we're going to expand our canvassing efforts to this area now as well. Now, I need to ask, how certain are you that this ribbon belongs to your daughter?"

"Very! I have more of the ribbon at home that matches this fabric. This is my daughter's!"

I look around the dark alley. What was she doing here? Tears begin to form again. It's something I'm getting used to tonight. I'm surprised I have any more water left in my body.

"This is a good discovery," the detective tells me. "Well done."

"Did you find her?" I turn and my husband is storming into the alley, pushing past several officers. "I'm the girl's father. Get out of my way!" They do, and he comes right up to us. "Don't tell me you found her in this alley? My God."

"No," Falls answers. "Your wife found your daughter's hair ribbon here."

"Where is it? Where was it found?"

Tears fall freely as I point to the pile of trash. "In the corner there," I tell him.

Roger is about to go look for himself when the detective puts a hand on his chest. "We're having a forensic team come and do tests now. If there's any more evidence of anything in this alley, we're going to find it, but you can't compromise that. That will hurt this investigation."

Roger attempts to calm himself. He suddenly starts taking shallow breaths. "That piece of trash, the child predator. Jeremy, does he live around here?"

Detective Falls slowly nods. "He does."

"Well, what the hell are we doing here?" he demands. "We need to go right now and talk to him. Kick his door down. My daughter is with him, isn't she? Oh, God."

Detective Falls tries to reason with him. "No, Mr. Bradshaw, you cannot speak to him directly. That's what we're going to do, immediately. But I can't have you come. If things get out of control, we could hurt this investigation. You don't want them to get away, right? So let me do my job."

"Let us do something though!"

"What child predator?" I say, confused.

"I showed your husband a bunch of photos of known criminals who target children, and he believes he saw one a few days ago in a park near the daycare." She turns to my husband. "Now, that doesn't necessarily mean anything. That doesn't mean this person is involved in what happened here. If you want to help my officers with canvassing this new area, I'll have you talk to them, and they'll tell you how you can help. Please, Mr. Bradshaw, it's best that you stay calm."

Roger paces around the alley, unable to speak.

"Child predator," I repeat. My imagination is running wild. I fall to my knees and begin weeping uncontrollably. Detective Falls runs over to me and attempts to console me. Roger continues pacing, collecting his own thoughts.

When I finally manage to stop and calm myself briefly, I call out for my husband. "Roger, please, just take me home. I can't do this anymore tonight."

"That's a good idea," Detective Falls says. "I'll call you if there's any update."

Roger points a finger. "Why are you still here? You need to go to that freak's house right now!"

"I'm working on a search warrant as we speak," the detective says. She puts her hand up. "I'm doing the best I can."

"Roger, take me home," I tell him again.

Roger wraps his arm around me and guides me out of the alley to where he's parked. He opens the door for me, and I sit inside. He closes the door more harshly than needed before getting into the driver's seat. He strikes the steering wheel several times.

"Roger," I say, trying to calm my husband.

He stops and turns on the ignition. The car radio turns on and immediately I hear beeping sounds from the station.

"This is an Amber Alert. This is a child abduction

emergency. Gracie Brad—"

Roger quickly turns off the radio and turns to me, tears of his own now coming down his face.

CHAPTER 24

Sarah

From the bedroom, I hear muffled shouting outside. Somehow I managed to fall asleep despite the chaos around me. Roger isn't in bed beside me now.

That's when I hear him curse outside the bedroom.

I get out of bed and open the door quietly. I slowly walk towards the kitchen, taking in every word I hear from my husband. I worry any update will be a bad one.

Whatever's happening now isn't good.

"What do you mean?" he shouts into his cell. "How does that happen?" He looks up and his furious face lightens when he sees me. He tightens his bottom lip and turns away. "How does no one in that area not see a four-year-old walking in an alley by herself?" He stops and listens a moment before shaking his head. "Tell me that guy's address. I'll search it myself!" He pauses again before his face erupts with rage. He ends the call and whips his cell phone into the couch.

"What happened?" I ask, confused.

"They talked to the scumbag. Jeremy Timmons. Detective Falls says they couldn't secure a search of his home, and the bastard says he won't speak to the police. He wouldn't allow them to search without a warrant. Can you believe this guy?"

"What did Detective Falls say? How are they going to find Gracie?"

"They're going to keep collecting evidence from the alley. If anything new comes up that points towards that sick piece of trash, she can secure a search of his property. She says she couldn't get a judge to sign off on a warrant because the ribbon was too far away from his residence. In the meantime, they have eyes on his property and they're talking to his neighbors. No one has seen Gracie, though."

I think of the bar's back entrance when I was in the alley. "What about camera footage from the alley? They must have footage of her, right?"

My husband shakes his head. "Falls checked with the bar already. That camera isn't functional. Just a damn deterrent. So we have nothing."

He walks past the table and smacks a saltshaker off it. It flies across the room, reminding me of the plate that shared a similar fate not too long ago.

Roger takes a deep breath. "How the hell does a little girl just disappear like this?" He leans against the table too much and it shifts across the floor. Roger stands up, trying to regain his balance.

Roger suddenly looks at me and goes to the living room, picking up several pictures from the coffee table. He comes back and drops them on the kitchen table, waving me over. "Take a look," he says. He sorts through them and picks one up. "Him. This is the guy. Jeremy Timmons. Do you remember him? I'm not going crazy, right? I saw this guy at the park that day I gave you the flowers. Do you remember him?"

I look at the picture. I look at his rough face and nose. Immediately I get an uneasy feeling about him, but I don't remember him.

I reluctantly shake my head. "I don't think so. I'm not sure."

Roger's bottom lip stiffens again. "Well, I do. I saw him. He was there. Sitting at the bench like the freak he is."

"Aren't these kinds of people barred from being around parks or schools?"

Roger nods. "Detective Falls says he lives just far enough that he's outside of the areas he's not supposed to be. He's also denying that he was at the park, but I saw him." He points a stern finger at me.

I grab his hand and try to console him. "I believe you. What do we do?"

"I'm going to find out where this trash lives. Kick his door in if I must. I don't care what the police do to me after. I don't care what it takes." He looks at me, his face full of rage and his eyes watery. "Whatever it takes, we're going to find Gracie."

CHAPTER 25

Annie

I put the kettle on the stove to make some nighttime tea. I always find it calms me before going to bed. I'm an anxious person, and sleep doesn't come easy. Sleep apps, melatonin, I've tried many things. It doesn't matter what I do, I'll only have a few hours of rest at night.

It's been like this since I was a child.

Mother would make me tea when I couldn't sleep. She attempted to comfort me when I needed it.

Just as I did for Gracie tonight. She had a hard time sleeping in the room. The smiling sun bothered her until she managed to drift off. I sat beside her bed, reading more than the four books I'd promised.

I even sang her some nighttime songs that Mother sang to me as a child. That helped.

When she asked if she could call Sarah to say goodnight to her mother, I lied again. I told her that Mom was out with her dad. It was their date night. After all, that's why we're having our little sleepover.

Tomorrow I'll have to lie again when she asks when her mom is picking her up. The day after will be another lie, and on it will go.

I realize I don't have an end plan on what to do. I acted on impulse and didn't plan.

That was another one of my mother's rules. Plan.

She had an end goal, but it's something I refuse to do. I won't do it. I'm not her.

Gracie needs me to save her, not make things worse.

No matter what good mothers have done for others, I'm not sure their kids' lives were better for it. I know mine isn't better after what my mother did for me.

I can't sleep. I'll never be able to sleep.

The kettle starts to whistle, and I take it off the burner, pouring the hot water into my mug.

Gracie is happy right now, but eventually she'll get sad, like the others. The children always get upset, especially when they realize they won't be seeing their mothers.

I take in a deep breath.

I remind myself that these are the fun times. Gracie still completely trusts everything I say.

Still, it bothers me how upset she is in the room. I didn't think she would hate the mural I painted of the sun as much as she does. When I painted it with Mother, it was meant to make the children happy.

She's scared, though.

If only she knew the horrors that happened in the room that's beside her, she would feel lucky to be in the one she's in.

A knock on my front door startles me. I tip my hand and tea spills on my fingers. My skin burns and I put it under water quickly. The person at the door knocks again, harder this time.

For a moment, I worry it will wake Gracie, but I remember how soundproof the room is. Mother ensured a long time ago that anyone at the front door would have a difficult time hearing someone in the basement.

Especially when the bookshelf was moved to its proper place.

Of course, the bookshelf isn't in the proper place.

The person at the door knocks again.

I quickly go to my door and open it slightly. A tall man in a police uniform nods at me.

"Evening, miss," he says to me. "I'm in your area speaking to your neighbors about a missing child." He squints at me a moment and suddenly realizes who I am. "Wait, you're the teacher, right?"

I nod. "Early childhood educator, we like to call ourselves. Gracie is my student." I almost expect the officer to burst through my door and demand I tell him where the girl is. Instead, he gives me a concerned look.

"Are you doing okay?" he asks.

"As best I can. Have there been any updates?"

He nods. "We found a red hair ribbon in an alley not too far from here. We're hoping to find someone who may have seen her."

He takes a step closer, and for a moment I worry that he'll ask to search my home. The bookshelf hasn't been moved. It wouldn't be hard for anyone to find the secret rooms. It wouldn't be hard to find Gracie sleeping.

How could I forget Mother's rule? Always put the bookshelf back every time you leave the rooms. Never allow an opportunity for someone to discover what you've done.

I've been more than sloppy with her rules since taking Gracie. There was a reason Mother was never caught, and that was because of her rules. I may not want to be like her, and what she's done, but like her, I never want to be caught.

"I just wanted to say," the officer says in a softer tone,

"I'm sorry to hear your mother isn't well. I only met her once. She retired soon after I started on the force."

I give a thin smile. "Thanks. Seems like my mother was well respected."

"She organized our station so well that we still use all of her systems today." He looks down at my dress and the bird prints on it. "Do you love working with children?"

I smile. "I do."

CHAPTER 26

Sarah

In the morning, Roger and I are back at the daycare, sitting at a small table. Mabel is leaning against a wall closest to the door. Detective Falls has been showing us video footage for nearly an hour, reviewing details with us.

Roger is barely able to watch the screen. At times shaking visibly with anger, he's been having trouble grasping that something like this could even happen. I'm the opposite. I'm watching every detail. Gracie's gone and someone took her. Somewhere in this video could be something that tells us what happened.

So far, though, that hasn't been the case. All I see are images of my little girl, who should be at the daycare today but isn't. She's missing and it's the fault of the staff here.

I calm myself and try to concentrate on the detective's words.

"We can see from video footage that indeed Mr. Bradshaw was never parked in the lot," she says.

"Great," Roger says. "My daughter's been missing since yesterday afternoon and all we have is what I told you... yesterday afternoon. Perfect." He looks at me, and I try my best to keep my composure.

The detective continues. "Well, we last see Gracie in the video footage at three fifteen. This is about five minutes before Ms. Meadows left and Mabel took over care."

I take a moment to glance at the supervisor, who shares a look with me. I can read her mind. She's hating herself as much as she should. My little girl is gone, and something terrible has happened.

"Now," the detective says, "we don't see Gracie at any point after this. We know she isn't in the building when Mrs. Bradshaw came to pick her up. Mabel and her searched the building. My own constables did the same. So we can rule out that she's somewhere here. We also don't see any indication that someone took her. My belief is she left."

"Bullshit," Roger grumbles under his breath.

Detective Falls ignores his comment and continues. "She must have left through an area that doesn't have any camera coverage."

"She's four!" Roger shouts. "She's not some mastermind escape artist getting out of daycare. This is ridiculous."

Detective Falls nods in understanding. "We know that things haven't been well at home the past few days. Gracie was scared." She looks at my husband. "No one appears to have helped her get out. Now, what we don't know is what happened after. Video footage around the area doesn't show any signs of Gracie at all. No one that we spoke to saw her. We know that at some point Gracie was in the alley behind the local bar, though. Her hair ribbon was found by you." She looks at me. I lower my head in response. "Now, is there anyone in this area that she knows? Anyone you two have visited? Friends? Aunts or uncles?"

"No," I answer. I don't bother telling her that I have no social circle besides my husband and mother.

"This doesn't make any sense," Roger says. "The scumbag. The predator guy. What's going on with him?"

"We have no new evidence, but if we do, we'll look into that. The rest of our canvassing efforts haven't been fruitful either."

"So, what you're saying is you have nothing, right?" Roger huffs. "Ridiculous!" He points a finger at Mabel. "I'm going to sue this place until it's closed to protect all the other kids in this city!"

The supervisor doesn't respond. You can see on her face that she felt every word. A subtle knock on the door interrupts Roger's tirade and Annie Meadows slowly opens it.

"Can I speak with you?" she asks the supervisor.

"And you!" Roger yells. "I'm not done with anybody at this daycare! *Care!* I feel like none of you do! My girl is gone, and what have you done?"

Detective Falls looks at my husband. "We're all here, right now, trying to find her." That quiets him.

"What is it, Annie?" Mabel asks.

When she shyly enters the room, I remember one of the last images I have of Gracie. Watching my little girl walking away with Annie. I remember Annie's menacing smile when I told her I would be picking her up.

"I just… can't be here today," Annie says. "With what happened with Gracie and my mother."

"Great," Roger continues, "so much for us all being here working together to find my daughter." Detective Falls looks at my husband sternly. For a moment I see the glance of a hardened officer and not the empathetic detective who's been working with us.

"Ms. Meadows," Falls says, "go ahead. You can leave. I don't need to speak with you any more today about this. If I need anything, I'll visit you at your home. Give my best to your mom."

Annie glances at Mabel, who nods. Annie closes the door behind her, and I look at the detective.

"Do you two know each other?" I ask, surprised at Falls' comment to Annie.

The detective looks at me for a moment, then at the supervisor. "I used to work with her mom at the police station."

"Oh, great," I mutter. "You're sympathetic to one of the possible people who did this."

Detective Falls shakes her head. "Everyone at the station knows the Meadowses. That doesn't make me biased. If the evidence pointed to her, she'd be in cuffs, okay? Now, let's focus on what we actually have."

"Which is nothing," Roger says again. "We know that Jeremy lives near the alley where the ribbon was found. Kick in the door now! She's there. I know it!"

"We can't. As soon as I can get a search warrant, we will. I promise."

"What about Annie?" I ask. Detective Falls nearly rolls her eyes at my question. "Does she live near the alley where we found the ribbon?"

That seems to temporarily stump the detective. "I'll look into that."

"Please do," I say mockingly. "Let's see where the evidence points to now."

CHAPTER 27

Annie

I finish reading another book and close it. Gracie smiles at me as she finishes her grilled cheese sandwich. It's not the typical lunch I'd like to provide for her, but I was later coming back from the daycare than I thought I would be and knew she would be hungry.

"Another story?" I ask Gracie.

She shakes her head. "Can we do some more crafts?"

I give her a wide smile. "What a wonderful idea, sweet pea. Yes! Let's do that."

"I want to make a gift for my mommy," she says.

I give her a thin smile. Gracie was obsessed with giving just me her art gifts. Now, she wants to give her mom one. The whole reason she's here is because of her mother.

I take out a container with paper and colored pencils, and we each start making our own pictures. I tell her that I'm drawing one for her to keep. She tells me again that hers is for her mom.

As we draw, I think of the exchange I had at the daycare with her parents. Specifically her father. It's hard not to think about it since it was Gracie's gift to me that set me off to wanting her to stay with me.

The more I found out about Roger Bradshaw, the

more I worried for Gracie. I watch her as she makes a bunch of circles with her red pencil and begins drawing a stick figure on top of it. A smaller stick figure is beside the tall one.

"Is that you and mommy?" I ask. Gracie nods. "Sweet pea," I ask softly, and I ask her to lower her pencil. "The artwork you made for me, the one with your dad, do you remember it?"

"Is that the Monster Daddy picture?" she asks innocently.

"Yes," I say, "that one. Now that we're alone here, I need to ask you again, did Daddy ever hit you?"

She looks at me a moment and lowers her head.

"Gracie, it's okay. You can tell Ms. Meadows. I may not look like it but I'm really strong." I raise my arm and attempt to show a bicep. "See? So you don't have to be scared of Monster Daddy anymore."

"He didn't hit me," she says again. It's an answer she gave me before. I didn't believe her back then and I still don't believe her now.

"Did he hit you on the bum ever?"

"Sometimes," she says.

Okay, now she's opening up. "What about your face?" I ask, puckering my lips. "Did he ever hit you in the face?"

Gracie smiles at my silly face but shakes her head no. "He yells. He scares me. He scares Mommy."

I sigh. I'm starting to question what I've done. Mother had a set of rules for the children she wanted to save, but even that rule I seem to be breaking. Mother had to know that the parents were hitting the child before she ever took them.

From the moment, Gracie gave me her artwork, I knew something was wrong. I tried to question her, but she wouldn't answer. The reasonable part of me said to call Children's Aid. A protective officer could look into it.

Mother would tell me horror stories of parents in the system. Even with child protective officers involved, terrible things could happen to the children.

I didn't call Children's Aid. I tried my best to control my impulses to help.

That's when I saw Gracie at the park after daycare a few days ago. She flinched when her father embraced her. She was scared. You could tell by her facial reaction.

Scared she was going to be hit again. She wouldn't have to be scared with me here to protect her.

The next day, when Gracie was petrified to leave the daycare with her father, I made up my mind.

Sarah Bradshaw was no better than Roger.

She was either complicit in what her husband did or participated. Either way, Gracie couldn't stay with her parents anymore.

Children's Aid wouldn't cut it.

She needed actual help.

She needed me.

I ask Gracie again, "But Daddy never hits you?"

"Nope," she says. "Can I color again?"

I nod. "What about Mommy? Mommy ever hit you?"

Gracie shakes her head.

"Does Mommy scare you like Daddy does?"

Gracie shakes her head again as she turns the paper over and again starts making wide circles with a blue pencil this time.

I breath out, starting to feel foolish. "Has Daddy ever hit Mommy?"

Gracie finally stops coloring and looks at me. It takes her some time before she shakes her head, but this time, she's not as playful as she was with her other answers.

I smile, knowing I'm on to something. "Well, I'll take your empty plate upstairs," I say, grabbing her half-eaten grilled cheese and cup. "Are you still hungry? Do you want a snack?"

Gracie shakes her head. "No thank you," she answers politely.

"Be right back," I tell her. When I leave the room, I put back the piece of wood locking the door and head upstairs. Once I'm in the kitchen, I open a drawer and look at the piece of artwork Gracie gave me several days ago. The one that started everything. The image I haven't been able to get out of my mind since seeing it.

At the top of some stairs is a stick figure drawn in black. The lines are drawn thick, and the character appears to be shouting with its mouth open. At the bottom of the stairs are two stick figures colored pink. The taller one is on its knees and the smaller stick figure has its stick arm over the other, as if consoling her. Both the pink stick figures have frowny faces.

CHAPTER 28

Annie

Before leaving the room, I look back at the child sleeping soundly in the bed, her sweet face illuminated by the nightlight.

She fell asleep easily today for her nap.

No obsessive fears over the smiling sun on the wall near her. A few books while she nestled under the sheets and she drifted to sleep.

It's been some time since a child was in this room. So many advancements in childcaring since the last one rested in a bed as nicely as Gracie. I walk over to a nightstand near the door and confirm the baby monitor is still on. The receiver is on already on my kitchen table. It only has audio. I plan on buying a more modern one soon.

This will do for now though. When she wakes, I'll be able to hear her upstairs. I'll get a snack ready and come back.

I don't plan to leave her alone today. I don't like leaving the house with Gracie here. The room is entirely safe for her, but adult supervision is always required. Gracie's safety is of the utmost importance. That's why she's here, after all.

She wasn't safe with her parents.

Gracie has opened up to me. I've found out more of what happens in the Bradshaw home. At first, I was worried I had chosen the wrong child to be in this room, until she told me the truth.

It took time, and trust, but she told me.

Children who come from homes where they're exposed to trauma know that something isn't right. They just don't know how to explain it. It takes time for them to process it and explain what they've come to know as normal.

Gracie belongs here, with me.

Mother would be proud.

She would even be proud that, for a change, I'm following her rules.

I open the door and take one last glance over at Gracie resting peacefully. She will be much happier here. Safer. She doesn't have to be scared anymore.

I close the door and lock it.

That's when I hear a pounding sound. My heart stops for a moment, and I realize it's coming from my front door. My eyes widen.

I quickly move the bookshelf to conceal the opening to the rooms in the basement. I try to compose myself but the knock on the door gets louder. I stand next to a small window facing the front yard. Mother taped cardboard over it decades ago, but time has created openings where you can see.

From the side view of the front porch, I see exactly who's outside and my mouth nearly drops.

Detective Cassie Falls is pounding on my front door. With her dress shirt tucked into her jeans, she rests her hand on her gun belt. My heart starts beating faster and I begin to panic.

How long has she been outside for?

Mother should have put a baby monitor near the front door as well. How else would we know if someone was at the door? We never exactly had company though.

I quickly go to the dryer and turn it on. The sound of the uneven machine is loud and sure to get attention. If Cassie didn't know I was home, she knows now. I run up the stairs and open the front door.

"Detective Falls?" I say with a wide smile.

"Hey, Annie," she says coldly. Her neutral demeanor has me worried already. No smile. No warm greeting. Why is she here?

"Sorry, I was in the bathroom." I laugh.

"I'm sorry to bother you at home," she says.

We stare at each other a moment, and the tension is palpable.

"How can I help you?" I ask, leaning against the door, blocking the inside of my house with my tiny body.

"I was hoping we could talk," she says.

I nod quickly. "Of course."

She gives a thin smile. "Well, can we talk inside?"

"Of course, silly me. Come inside." I open the door wide and the detective walks into the living room, looking around.

If she had the power to read minds, she would see how frantically mine is racing. I'd already be in handcuffs. She sits on the couch.

A coughing sound comes from the kitchen. My heart stops when I realize it's the baby monitor.

How would I even explain something like that if the detective finds it? I may as well put out my hands and tell her to slap the cuffs on.

"Is there someone else here?" she asks. "Do you have

company?"

My wide smile that has been concealing my worst fears disappears, showing my true expression. I quickly plaster a new smile on. "No, just the radio. Sometimes I like to put it on when I do chores. Tea?" I say frantically. She shakes her head, but I tell her I'll get her some anyway.

I turn and pray that Gracie doesn't wake up in the next few seconds. All it would take is another loud cough, her to say a word, and everything comes to an end.

Thankfully, my house is not open concept. Once inside the kitchen, the detective can't see me, and I quickly turn off the baby monitor and hide it in a drawer. A wave of relief washes over me.

Even if Gracie calls out now, the detective likely won't be able to hear her. The room is soundproof. The loud dryer will also help conceal any sounds as well. The measures Mother took to not be discovered are saving me.

"How's your mom?" the detective asks.

"Not doing well," I say from the kitchen. I'm trying to collect myself before I show my face in the living room again.

Detective Falls walks into the kitchen and looks at me intensely. "I lost my father over a year ago," she says. "It was the hardest time of my life. I know it's just you in the house now, but if you ever need someone to talk to, I'm here."

I smile. "And I know where to find you." I point outside. "About two blocks that way."

"Your mom always had an easy commute to work. Listen, I know you spoke to an officer of mine the other night when they were knocking on doors, but I was hoping we could talk again."

"No problem. What's on your mind?"

"Well, we have a lead in Gracie's disappearance. Her hair tie was found in an alley nearby. The only person Gracie knows in this area is you."

"Okay," I say nervously. I look past the detective at the kitchen table. This time my heart is about to explode out of my chest when I see a pile of artwork from Gracie on the table.

Stupid. Stupid.

How many mistakes can I make? I was planning on keeping them. She made them for me, after all. The ones she drew for her mom I already threw out.

"Because of the proximity of your home to where her ribbon was found and that you were the last person to talk to her, there are some concerns," Detective Falls says.

I look at her, stunned, as if she told me she knew I was the one.

She sighs. "I'm sorry to talk to you like this, I am, but you're the last person to see Gracie Bradshaw. I need to properly rule you out as a suspect."

"Okay," I say again. "I understand. What would you like to ask me?"

She gives a thin smile. "I don't really have any new questions for you. You've already answered them multiple times over. What I need is confirmation that you don't have Gracie in this house." She points down at the floor as she says the words, not knowing that the approximate place she's pointing is where Gracie is. "Can I search your home?"

"Um."

"I understand. This isn't how I would like to do this with you," she says. "A quick search, and I'll be out of your hair. I won't have to bother you like this anymore. Is that okay?"

I stare at her like a statue. Maybe if I don't move or breathe, she'll think I am one and just leave. When I realize I'm taking a longer time to respond, I finally manage to say something. "Of course," I say with a wide smile. "I completely understand your position."

She smiles back. "Great. I guess we can start with the kitchen." She laughs. "Obviously Gracie isn't here." She quickly glances around and notices the pile of artwork on the table. She picks one up and stares at it intensely.

My expression drops, and I wait for her to realize who made it.

"How can you pretend to like the art that these children make you?" she asks with a laugh. "You have so many too."

I nervously smile again and shrug my shoulders. "Comes with the job."

She picks up another and looks at both pictures. "You have an artist on your hands here."

"The children love to give me gifts," I say in a hushed voice. All those gifts were from Gracie specifically. I breathe in deep when the detective looks at a third picture of two pink colored stick figures. She takes her time examining them and suddenly drops them back on the table.

"Can we look upstairs?" she asks.

I compose myself and head out of the kitchen and walk up the stairs with the detective closely behind. After she looks in both bedrooms, she closes the doors, and we head back downstairs.

I walk towards the front door. "If you ever do have any more questions, let me know," I say.

The detective smiles at me. "You have a basement too,

right?" I can hear the loud dryer from main floor, so the answer is already assumed.

"Right," I say. "You'd probably like to see downstairs as well. This way." I gesture back towards the kitchen. I open a small door at the end and walk slowly down the stairs. Each step is reluctant knowing that once we're in the basement, I'll be exposed.

The rooms will be discovered. Gracie will be seen.

She'll be forced to go back to her parents. Forced to be scared. She'll be hurt.

As I set foot on the cold concrete, Detective Falls looks around. The dryer is banging unevenly against the floor. Even though the rooms are soundproof, if Grace were to start kicking against the door, the detective could hear.

Detective Falls paces around the large, unfinished basement, taking more time to examine the surroundings than any other room in the house prior. It's as if she can smell something is off down here.

She walks over to the bookshelf.

Behind it are the rooms. Behind it is Gracie.

All I can do is watch as I'm about to be discovered. Instead, the detective picks up one of the books. "I've actually read this one," she says. She places it back on the shelf and turns to me. "Thanks again, Annie. I appreciate you letting me look around your home. That makes things so much easier. You didn't have to let me inside."

I didn't? I didn't know that was an option. I suppose I couldn't scream at her to go away and leave me alone though.

"But," she says, "of course I didn't expect you to say no. You have nothing to hide."

The dryer suddenly stops working, and the entire basement is now quiet. Inside, my mind is racing again.

"Well, I was planning on visiting my mother now," I say quickly.

"Of course," she says, starting up the stairs.

CHAPTER 29

Sarah

I sit in my car and wait. I've been waiting for hours.

Sometimes you know something is off, and my gut is yelling at me that Annie Meadows is more than just an odd daycare teacher.

There was always something about her that bothered me. Part of it was how good Gracie was with her. It was as if I was jealous that Annie was a better mother than me.

I shrug off those feelings. Something is off. She was the last person to see Gracie. I don't have a way to explain why Annie was still on the daycare camera footage even after Gracie was last seen though. If Annie helped Gracie leave the building, wouldn't they have gone at the same time?

Then I found the hair ribbon in the alley. Annie lives near there.

I pleaded for Detective Falls to investigate this more. She explained that an officer did talk to Annie last night. That's not good enough. The detective said she would look into it more; call me crazy but I don't trust her enough to do so.

Detective Falls and Annie know each other.

Roger thinks I'm obsessed. Annie Meadows is a strange young woman, he agrees, but doesn't see what I do. He doesn't have the same gut feelings I have. His are leading him down a different route.

As obsessed as I am with Annie Meadows, he is with this ex-con. It's hard to disagree with his logic, though. A child predator makes more sense than a daycare teacher.

As I sit in my car and stare at the building, I know I'm taking this too far. I'm back to my old private investigation ways.

Annie Meadows has something to do with Gracie going missing. I know it. I just have no evidence. I don't know anything about the young woman. I don't know where she lives. All I know is she has a creepy smile, wears dresses with stupid kid patterns on them every day and is obsessed with my daughter.

I know about her mother though. She's sick, dying actually. In a respite home, waiting to take her last breath.

There's only one unit like this in the city. I called and asked if a Ms. Meadows was there. They confirmed she was, and I quickly asked what visiting hours are and ended the call. Thankfully the receptionist didn't ask me for Annie's mother's first name.

Since that phone call, I've been sitting in my car parked close by the hospital. It's been over two hours. I'm hungry, thirsty and have to pee. None of that matters until I see that awkward woman on her bicycle come by.

Once I see her, I'll follow her home. I'll know where she lives. I can then do my own investigation.

My phone rings and I quickly answer it. "Hello?" I say, as I stare outside.

"It's Detective Falls."

"Did you talk to Annie again?" I ask.

"I did," she says. "I even searched her home. Gracie isn't there."

"She let you search her home?" I say, confused.

"That's right," the detective says. "I know you have your concerns about Ms. Meadows, but I hope this alleviates them."

I realize I've stopped breathing and take a big breath. "Well, that doesn't mean anything. She could be keeping her somewhere else."

I can almost hear the detective sigh over the phone. "I really don't think Annie Meadows has anything to do with what's happened, Sarah."

"Of course not," I say. "You're best friends with her mother, right?"

"I did what you asked," she says. "I investigated it more. It's a dead end. I think we need to focus on other things."

A wide smile comes across my face as I spot a woman on a bicycle coming up the road. Annie Meadows puts her bike in a rack outside the building.

"You focus on those things," I say to the detective. "I'll do my own investigation." I end the call before she can say another word.

CHAPTER 30

Roger

"Sarah, call me back when you get this." I end the call on my cell phone and toss it on the passenger seat. Where is she? She hasn't answered a call or text from me in the past two hours. She was supposed to meet me at the park across from the daycare an hour ago. We both wanted to do our own things today while looking for Gracie.

I think part of it was we both needed our space. Tensions are high and so are emotions. I feel like I'm on the verge of breaking down in tears or wanting to smash something.

Right now, I'm leaning towards breaking something.

Sarah was supposed to meet me at the park, and she's nowhere in sight. Does she think what she's doing is more important than what we agreed to do together?

I have a stack of missing person posters I printed out and we were going to tape them around anything we could in the neighborhood. We decided to start around the daycare and work our way to the alleyway where the ribbon was found. After that, if we had time, we'd expand around the city as much as we could.

I was the one skeptical at first. Esta isn't that large. Most people likely heard about the missing girl. Sarah pointed out that many may not know what she looks like though.

I even put a cash reward on the poster. Ten thousand dollars to anybody whose information leads to her safe return.

I don't have ten thousand. Sarah's parents don't have that type of money either. I'll deal with that problem if someone comes up. Part of me would wonder if any claimant was involved anyway.

Despite this not being my idea, I agreed to create and print the posters. Sarah, who has talked non-stop about Annie Meadows all day, is now nowhere to be found.

She has her person of interest and I have mine. The more logical suspect. Jeremy Timmons. A child predator who targets little girls.

I begin coughing and have trouble catching my breath. I roll down my car window, suspecting I'm about to lose my lunch. I take deep breaths and feel better.

I can't stop thinking where Gracie may be and who may have her. What they could be doing to her.

This is a nightmare.

Thankfully, I have a solid idea who's behind it all. I'm waiting for a call that will confirm what I need to know to find out for myself.

For hours I've been driving around the neighborhoods close to the alley and the daycare. Every so often, I'll call Detective Falls for an update. She never has one.

It's hopeless.

I grip the steering wheel and curse to myself. "Where the hell is Sarah?" I shout out loud. I start banging on the steering wheel. I try to calm myself by lowering my head on the wheel. My car beeps, making an elderly couple jump while walking on the sidewalk beside me. I wave at them to apologize.

Jeremy Timmons.

I've never felt so right about something in my entire life. It's a weird situation. I want to be right, but pray I'm wrong. If he had something to do with what happened to my daughter, she may not be alive.

I tried my best to find out as much as I could about Jeremy, but found nothing online. Detective Falls told me the charges he went to jail for. The thought of the images he had on his laptop made me sick to my stomach.

Somehow I know that that's not the end of it. He likely did worse than what he went to jail for.

And yet this piece of garbage gets to be "rehabilitated" and walk the streets with other people. He should be nowhere near children, ever. Yet I found him near a playground. One that was across the street from my daughter's daycare.

I shudder at the idea.

Detective Falls wouldn't tell me where he lived, so I took it upon myself to find out.

As if the universe heard my plea, my phone rings and when I look at the display, I have an authentic smile on my face for the first time in a while.

"Hey," I say. "It's Roger." I'm thrilled the private investigator finally called. "Please tell me you have an address."

"I'm sorry how long this took, but I had to double check a few things to make sure. The home isn't in his name, but I have an address."

"Thank God," I say. I write down the address and double check I have it right before ending the call. It may have cost a lot to involve a private investigator, but it will be worth every penny if I find my little girl.

I immediately put the address on my GPS in my car. I'm only minutes away. I call Sarah again, but this time it goes straight to voicemail. "Sarah! Call me back as soon as you can." I hang up as I get closer.

Pure adrenaline is pumping through my body, and I still have no clue what I'm going to do when I get to the pervert's house. I imagine booting down the door, kicking his ass, and searching the home.

What if he calls the cops, though?

That wouldn't matter. All I would have to do is find Gracie. If I do find my little girl, good, let the police come. I'll have a lot of explaining to do though if she's not.

I try and imagine multiple ways I can handle this, but all of them end up with me pummeling the pervert's face in.

I start to crawl as I look at the numbers on the houses until I spot the one I was given. The single-floor home is clearly not cared for.

A window in the front is boarded up. There's a large hole in one of the wooden stairs leading to the porch. The roof has broken shingles. The off-colored yellow exterior vinyl panels are stained with multiple colors. It would be a power washer's dream to clean the outside.

The home even looks like it belongs to a child predator.

After all the ways I imagined this going, I never thought I'd follow through with the simplest.

I knock on the door and wait impatiently for someone to answer.

I only wait a few moments before knocking harder on the door. Still nobody comes. I clench my fist.

Unreal.

After all of this, the perv isn't home.

I look around the neighborhood and don't see anybody nearby. I grip the door handle and attempt to open it.

Locked. Of course. What did I expect?

I go to the front window and peer inside. The shades are shut but I can see a light from a lamp. Beside it is a recliner and a beer on the nightstand.

I take a deep breath. Gracie could be inside this house right now.

Or she could be with Jeremy somewhere else. I try not to let those thoughts get to me. Instead, I refocus on getting inside.

She could be in one of these rooms, scared for her life. If she's not here, there could be evidence of his involvement somewhere.

I attempt to open the front window, but it's locked as well. I look around the empty street before walking around the house, checking the windows. Everything is locked tightly.

When I get into the backyard I'm disgusted by the care of the grass. It looks like it hasn't been mowed in months. The entire backyard is in disarray. A pile of rocks and wood is against one side of the decrepit fence that surrounds the property.

I walk up to the back door and attempt again to enter, but it's locked. I look through a small window in the door, but see no movement.

It's evident that Jeremy isn't home.

That only encourages me to break in.

I take my elbow and smash it into the windowpane. I hear a small crack when I do, and wince in pain. I look down at my arm and see a cut.

I realize I'm doing this all wrong but forgive myself

quickly since I'm not the type to break into people's homes. I walk over to the pile of rocks. This time, I break the glass without further injury. I use the rock and drag it around the windows edges before reaching in and attempting to unlock the door.

After a few moments I feel vulnerable. All it would take is a sensible neighbor wondering what's happening next door to call the police on me. My worries vanish when I feel the lock and open the door. I quickly enter the house and take a deep breath.

Part of me wants to yell out for my daughter. Instead, I start looking around. Dirty dishes are stacked in the sink and the counter space beside it. Used pots and pans are on the stove. Pizza boxes are packed on top of a small recycle bin. That's when I smell the combined aroma of the bachelor's lifestyle.

I feel dirty just being inside.

I begin my search in the kitchen, looking through cabinets and drawers. I push the pizza boxes off the bin and look inside, and then the garbage. Next I go into the living room, but again find nothing. There's no upstairs and only two bedrooms. There appears to be no basement as well.

I look in one of the rooms. Pictures of young-looking Asian cartoon characters are postered on the wall. Clothes are piled high in a corner. A computer and desk are on the other side. There's an odor of piss.

I immediately know this is Jeremy's room. Again, I'm sick to my stomach and feel like destroying his home. I calm myself and try looking through dresser drawers and the closet. I find nothing, and thankfully nothing that I suspected I would have in the home of a child predator.

I'm about to open the next bedroom door when I hear

a faint voice from inside.

"Jeremy?" a frail voice shouts.

I stop myself from entering.

"Son, is that you?" the older man asks. I take a few steps back, trying as best I can to be quiet.

"Who's there?" the frail voice asks.

I cover my mouth and try holding my breath.

A voice inside me tells me to open the door. This person may be Jeremy's father, but my daughter could be inside. Do perverts work together?

I breathe in deep and cover my face with my sweater as best I can. When I enter the room, an older man is laying on a small bed. His wrinkled face is full of fear when he sees me. A cane is leaned against the bed.

I quickly look around the room and see no indications that a little girl was there. I spot the closet and walk up to it.

"Don't hurt me!" the old man pleads. "Please!"

I ignore him and open the closet door. Nothing.

"Please," the old man says, his eyes watery.

I look at him coldly. "Where's the girl?"

"What?" he says, confused. He puts a hand to the middle of his chest. "Please, leave me alone. Take what you want. We don't have much."

"Where's the little girl you took?"

The man looks frightened and confused, and he begins coughing again. He curls in a ball on his bed and sounds like he's in pain.

"What?" I ask, confused myself. "You're not having a heart attack. Oh, God." I remind myself why I'm here and focus again. "Where's the child Jeremy took?"

The old man continues to cough and groans in pain. I begin to realize the mistake I've made.

CHAPTER 31

Annie

After Detective Falls leaves my home, I decide to follow through with what I said I was doing.

I have to visit my mother.

Now is not the time to do something that could be taken the wrong way. If I don't leave my house, and Detective Falls is still outside in her vehicle, she could suspect something.

That is if she doesn't suspect something already.

She looked at the pile of drawings Gracie made for me. All of them looked the same. Terrible circles and even worse stick figures with feet but no hands.

I had even pointed out Gracie's artwork to Cassie at the daycare.

She could have easily put it together.

I remind myself that Gracie is a heavy napper. At daycare she was always the last to wake, and it was because we had to force her to. She could easily have continued sleeping.

Now that I know what things are like in the Bradshaw house, I understand why she's tired. The little girl gets no sleep. She's probably scared for her life.

I step off my front porch and grab my bicycle. As I do, I look around the neighborhood but thankfully can't see

Detective Falls.

I carry my bicycle to the sidewalk and quickly make my way to the Rosewood hospice unit. It usually takes me fifteen minutes to get there.

I'll go see Mother and come right back. A quick visit.

Part of me wants to see her today. Not only because she doesn't have much time left on earth, but because after my time with Gracie, I understand my mother better.

I understand why she did the things she did.

I finally understood the rules she had for her conduct.

One of them, that I refused to follow, was she wouldn't just take a child, but the entire family. Mother, father, and the child or children.

Typically, she would allow the mother to stay with their child, unless she suspected the mother abused their kid as well.

The father would stay in the other room.

It's much smaller than the one Gracie's in. No bed. A cold concrete floor. No beautifully painted sky on the wall with a smiling sun.

Mother would usually let them sit in the dark, controlling the only light from outside the room.

The abuser would only see darkness, where they got to stay and think about what they'd done.

Mother already knew the terrible things they'd done. She read the reports when she worked at the police station. She saw the parents who got away with abuse. She read about the injuries the children had, many whose wounds lasted well beyond the physical recovery they needed.

That's when my mother couldn't stand aside any longer. Something had to be done. She was the one to do it.

After all, she understood well what growing up in a home like that was like for a child. She never wanted me to suffer that.

She did what she had to do.

Mother only chose families where she could confirm that abuse was occurring through police reporting.

Rule one. Don't chase anyone who can be traced back to you. Mother broke that rule once and understood why you should never do it again. It was too risky.

Rule two. Only choose children to save when you confirm they need saving. That was easy for her to do with her job.

In my occupation, I suspected it at times. It was only when Gracie gave me her drawing of her father that I knew something had to be done.

Rule three. Young children only. It was better this way.

Rule four. Know your own limits. I'm a petite woman and my mother wasn't much stronger. A man could easily overpower her. Once the father is locked in the small, dark room, never open the door, ever.

They could hurt you and easily escape.

Only open the slot at the bottom of the door to give food to them. Never talk to them, ever.

Abusers can be sweet-talkers. They can charm their way into your heart, only to destroy it. Once they have you in their power, they'll do with you what they want. That can happen if you pay attention to them.

Any time my mother had her doubts of what she was doing, she would look at the reports of what the men, mostly, had done.

Mother enjoyed reminding the men in the locked

room why they were there as well. Every so often, she would turn on the light in the room, open the slot at the bottom and slide in the police reports. The men would get enough time to read what they did.

Remind themselves why they deserve to be where they were. She'd turn off the lights immediately after.

She never opened the door for them. Once they were inside, they stayed.

The only time you open the door is after they've starved to death and it's time to conceal their body.

Rule five. Break the other parent.

When a mother lives in an abusive home, at some point they lose their sense of what's right and wrong and substitute it for what the abuser wants. They're living in their world, where the abuse they receive is normal.

It's not. It never is. They need to re-learn this.

Rule six. Once they understand, they can be free.

It always amazed me how Mother was never caught once the mother and child were allowed to leave. All they had to do was report her.

They never did.

The mother and daughter were blindfolded when they left. Mother would drive them to a new location and drop them off safely.

The children were often too young to understand what had happened, which was what Mother wanted, and was why she only chose young children.

The mothers did remember, though. I always wondered why they wouldn't tell the police. Some women, once free, would even thank my mother for what she'd done.

They could be themselves again.

A person.

Not an object that was owned and easily tormented and controlled by their abusers.

Not only were the children saved, but so were they.

When I was older, Mother began sharing details to me, reading the police reports of what the father had done to not only the wife, but the child too.

Still, I felt murder was too much.

The last man Mother starved to death in the room, she allowed me to help her dispose of the body. My reaction to what we were doing was enough for her to stop. She never wanted to put me through that again.

No matter how many children and mothers she would save by continuing, it wasn't worth putting her child through more.

I had suspected she wanted to stop as well. Especially after the body of one of the men who died in our basement was found.

It was only a matter of time before we were discovered. It was only a matter of time before police knocked on our door.

It had already happened twice to me in two days.

That was because I didn't follow the rules.

I thought I could get away with not killing. I didn't want to have Sarah or Roger in my basement. I only wanted to save Gracie.

I arrive at the medical building and park my bicycle on the rack outside the entrance. I quickly head to Mother's room.

Inside, her nurse, Melanie, is taking her blood pressure. Mother looks much worse than before. After Melanie finishes, she jots down some numbers on her notepad.

"What's happening?" I ask.

The nurse gives me a worried look. "She could pass tonight. I'm so sorry."

I nod at her before she leaves the room. I look at what's left of my mother on the bed and hold back my tears. I kneel on the floor beside her and grab her hand softly. Her skin is cold. I feel a tear rolling down my cheek. I kiss her forehead and I'm taken aback by how much colder her head feels from her hand.

"Mother," I say to her softly. "I hope you can hear me. I need you to know, I get it now." I stare at her face. She's not moving. Likely she can't hear anything I say. I hope she can, though. "I'm sorry, Mother. I was wrong. I hated you for a long time for killing them. I thought it was wrong." I breathe out deeply. "I thought I could do this without hurting anyone. I should have followed your rules from the start. I was wrong... You were right."

Her hand moves in mine, and I smile. "You can hear me, can't you?" I take a deep breath. "You'd be proud of me. I've saved a child. You would love her. Her name's Gracie. She's four years old." I wait with anticipation for her to open her eyes and talk to me, but she doesn't. "I can't stay. I'm sorry. If you were able to talk to me, I know you'd understand. I shouldn't have left Gracie, but I had to see you." I kiss her hand. "I love you, Mother. Goodbye."

I stand up, and walk out of her room, maintaining my composure and fighting the urge to look back at her. If I do, I'll stay much longer than I should. Gracie needs me. When I leave the building, I get back on my bicycle and ride faster back home.

I'm worried Gracie may have woken up. If she has, she'll be scared in the basement by herself. I peddle faster. I'm only a few blocks away from my house now but must stop at an intersection.

While I wait impatiently, I spot a man in a grey sweater on the other side. I stare at him and realize I've seen his face before.

I've seen a picture of this man many times. The man with the crooked nose on the bulletin board.

He was one of the bad men who also hurt children.

I grind my teeth to the point where I feel pain in my jaw.

The light turns green, and the man starts to walk across the street towards me. All I can do is stare at him.

How I would love for him to be in my basement. I would love nothing more than to put him in the small, dark room and lock the door. It would be a pleasure to dispose of his body.

As he passes me, he stares at me coldly. "What?" he says with a tone. I stand up, my bicycle between my legs, and imagine running into him with it. Instead, he keeps walking past me.

I turn my head to watch him leave. When I do, I notice something else. In a car right behind me is someone else I recognize. A woman I know well.

CHAPTER 32

Sarah

I can barely contain myself as I continue to follow Annie Meadows on her bicycle. I know these streets well now that I've been searching them aimlessly for any signs of Gracie. I know that the alley where I found her hair ribbon is nearby,

That means Annie Meadows' house is nearby.

When she stops at an intersection, I quickly park at the side of the road. For a moment I'm worried that she's spotted me. She's not moving any more.

When did she see me? My phone buzzes on the passenger seat. I quickly glance at it and see its Roger. Before I can answer, Annie resumes cycling across the street. I ignore my husband's call to continue to follow her.

After what feels like forever, Annie begins to slow and stops entirely in front of a house. She carries her bicycle up some steps and leaves it on the porch. She takes out her keys and unlocks the door. I watch as the young woman enters the house and closes the door behind her.

I'm nearly shaking with adrenaline. Now what?

Detective Falls told me she searched Annie's house; what else can I discover? I'm not a detective. I'm just a mother. I think of calling Roger, confused about what to do next.

Before I pick up my phone, Annie comes out of her house again and quickly grabs her bicycle. She nearly runs down the steps with it and jumps back on, riding furiously down the road.

Where is she going now?

In her haste, I realize she's left the door partially open. She never locked it.

I look at my rear-view mirror and can see Annie peddling down the street, the image of her getting smaller and smaller.

I glance at the front door and immediately feel an urge to go inside.

Now's the perfect time to do it. Annie left. It's unlocked.

Sure, Detective Falls searched the home, but she could have missed something. Police officers said they searched the alleys, and yet I was the one to find Gracie's hair ribbon.

The detective is also fond of Annie. That much is evident. She could have allowed her relationship with Annie's mother to compromise her judgement.

I quickly get out of my car and look around the neighborhood. It's daytime and still during work hours. The street is essentially barren, except for an elderly couple walking down it.

I ascend the steps to Annie's front door and reluctantly enter the house.

I peer around the living room. A mug with a tea bag is on the side table beside a book. A large portrait of Annie is on the wall. She looks to be about the same age she is now. She has her hands behind a large chair with an older woman sitting. Both are smiling.

Her mother. The one who's sick.

Annie just came back from the hospice. Maybe her mother isn't doing well to the point she had to go back.

Suddenly I feel guilt-stricken that I'm in this house. While a daughter hurries back to be by the side of her dying mother, I rummage through her home?

I hear a crackle in another room. I turn and realize it's coming from the kitchen.

"Hello?" I hear a faint voice call out. The voice is tired, but I immediately recognize it.

"Gracie?" I call out. "Gracie!"

I run into the kitchen and on the table is a baby monitor. The device lights up red, and again I hear her voice. "Hello?" she calls out. "Mrs. Meadows?"

"Gracie!" I yell. "Where are you?" I run upstairs and check both bedrooms, but find nothing. I run downstairs and hear the sweet voice of my angel again from the baby monitor in the kitchen.

"Can you hear me?" Gracie calls out.

Oh, I hear you. Thank God, I hear you. I go back into the kitchen and see another door. I open it and see it leads to the basement. I run down the stairs, nearly tripping over my feet. Once at the bottom of the stairs, I see a large bookshelf, and beside it, an opening.

I walk inside the area and see two doors. One is locked from the outside. The other is open, and a light is on inside.

"Gracie!" I yell. I walk into the room. It's small, and inside is a picture on the floor. I instantly realize who the artist is.

Two pink stick figures are standing on top of several circles. I go inside and pick it up, tears coming down my face.

The other room. Gracie's there. I'm about to call the police but realize that in my haste, I've left my cell in my car.

That doesn't matter. I need to save my daughter from whatever atrocities Annie has put her through.

I'm about to run out of the room when I find something blocking my exit.

Annie Meadows, with her creepy smile, is staring back at me. In her hand is a large kitchen knife that she pats against her white dress with ladybugs embroidered on it.

"You're not allowed to leave," she says coldly as she slams the door. I attempt to open it, but it's locked.

"Annie!" I shout. "Open this door! Gracie! Mommy's here!"

Suddenly, the light above me turns off.

CHAPTER 33

Roger

I tape a poster to a wooden power pole. I take a moment to stare at the beautiful face of my little girl before I move on to the next one.

I must stop doing that. Every so often I catch myself. It's going to be a long day if I weep at every missing person poster I put up.

Sarah should be here with me doing this; it's not fair she's making me do it myself. I've called her several more times, but it still goes straight to voicemail.

That would usually have me concerned, but not right now. Last time she was on her own, she found the hair ribbon.

This time, hopefully she'll find something else.

All I know is that I'm second-guessing Jeremy Timmons.

As I continue to walk around the neighborhood and reflect on what I've done today, it's hard not to think of the old man, Jeremy's father.

He seemed too frail to care for himself and likely completely depends on Jeremy for everything.

What a terrible life to have to rely on a person like that to live.

Still, the look of fear he had when I walked in his

room gets to me. The face he made when I talked to him. I thought he was going to die from a heart attack right in front of me.

I found nothing that confirmed Jeremy has Gracie. That doesn't mean he didn't do it. It just means he didn't take her to his home. Maybe he wouldn't do that out of fear of what his father would think.

I don't know.

I don't know anything anymore. I just want Gracie back.

I take out my cell and attempt again to call Sarah. I have several hundred more posters left and to hell if I'm doing them all myself.

Straight to voicemail again, which is now full. Likely all of the messages are me bitching about her not being here.

I call her mother, and thankfully she picks up. Unfortunately, she has no clue where her daughter is either.

I'm not sure where my wife is, but she should have at least texted me by now. Likely she's out there, searching alleys or doing whatever else she's doing and hasn't even noticed her phone's died.

My cell buzzes in my hand, and for a moment, I'm hopeful it's Sarah. I pick it up immediately.

"Hello," I say.

"It's Detective Falls."

"Any updates?" I ask immediately. Every time the woman calls, my heart stops and I anticipate bad news.

"Not about Gracie, no."

I lower my head and take a deep breath. "Have you heard from Sarah? She hasn't called me back in some time."

"I haven't seen her since this morning at the daycare," she says. There is something in her tone I don't like. Usually, she has a softer voice when she talks. She has a way of calming me even though I want to explode every other minute.

"Well, if she does call you, can you tell her to call me back?" I ask. I think of Annie Meadows. "Her phone goes straight to voicemail. She hasn't told me or her mom where she is. I'm starting to worry, I guess."

"Where do you think she is?" the detective asks, finally showing signs of her usual tone.

I breath in deep. "She's been obsessed about Annie Meadows since this morning. I mean, you heard her at the daycare today."

"I called her a few hours ago and let her know that I searched Annie Meadows' home personally. She voluntarily let me inside to look."

I nod. "That's good, I guess. I'm still worried."

"Where are you right now?" she asks, colder.

"Around the daycare. Putting up posters. I told you we'd be doing that today. That's another reason I'm worried. Sarah was supposed to help me with this."

"And that's okay," she says, "but what's not okay is you conducting a more aggressive investigation on your own."

I stop breathing for a moment. If she said this to me in person, there would be no way to hide how guilty I look.

"There was a break-in at Jeremy Timmons home. His father reported it to the police."

"Oh," I say. I realize I need to say very little, if anything.

"I find it more interesting that the invader didn't take

anything and threatened the old man to tell him where the little girl was."

"I see."

"The man is elderly and wasn't in good condition when police arrived."

I lower my head again. "Is he okay?"

"He had to be brought to the emergency room and I don't have any more updates right now on him. Unfortunately, he was not able to give a description of the invader. At least, not in the state he was in when he was found."

I feel my pulse quicken and my heart beats faster. "That's terrible."

The detective gives an audible sigh. "No more of your own investigations. Not like that, Mr. Bradshaw."

I feel a surge of rage. "I need to find Gracie! Someone needs to do something!"

"You're making this worse," she says coldly. "If the old man gives us a description, it won't be hard to put it together. This is the only warning you're going to get."

"No, this is my warning. Find. My. Daughter!"

CHAPTER 34

Sarah

"Gracie!" I pound on the door and walls and continue to scream for my child.

The room is dark and quiet, except for my screams and pleas for Annie to open the door. I'm not sure how long I've been in here.

In between my shouts, I break down in tears. When I get terrified, I remind myself that I found Gracie. She's here. The other room that was locked. She must be in there. She didn't sound scared when I heard her voice.

I've seen my daughter scared before. How many nights have I slept with her after a bad nightmare? How many cries have I consoled her through?

She's alive, and she's in a room right beside me.

I just can't speak to her.

"Gracie! Gracie! Gracie!"

I continue to shout as if any of my previous attempts helped.

"Please, Annie! Let me out. Let me see my daughter." I pace around the small room, my hands out, attempting to not hit the walls.

What does the woman have in store for me?

It's not entirely dark. The only light is the edge of a slot at the bottom of the door. I tried to open it and scream for help, but it too is locked from the outside.

"Annie!" I shout. "Open this door! I won't tell anyone what you've done. Just let Gracie and I leave, and I won't say a word."

When no one answers, I begin to cry again. "Open the door!"

Suddenly, the light bulb above my head turns back on. I close my eyes, unable to see clearly.

The slot at the bottom of the door opens, and I hear her voice. "Keys," she says coldly.

"What?"

"Put your keys through the slot." When I don't answer, she yells.

"Let me out," I say.

"Keys now! If you don't, bad things will happen."

I quickly dig into my jeans and toss the keys through the slot. "Okay. Please don't do anything. Can I see Gracie?"

"I'm not supposed to talk to you," Annie says.

I get down on my knees and look outside the room. I see Annie's legs and the bottom of her dress, and my keys on the ground.

"Annie, please," I plead. "Let me see her. Let me see Gracie. I just need to see my daughter."

"I'm not supposed to talk to you," she repeats. "It's the rules. I didn't make them. So I won't talk to you anymore."

"Annie! Just let me—"

A piece of paper flies through the slot. I pick it up and see it's one Gracie made.

A dark stick figure is shouting at the top of a flight of stairs. At the bottom are two pink stick figures with frowning faces.

"You don't deserve her," Annie says before closing the

slot.

"Wait! Annie!" I look up at the light, but this time it stays on. I try to calm myself and feel comforted that after a few minutes the light is still on.

Staying in the dark so long has been more than frightening. It's unbearable.

I look down at the picture Gracie made. I realize right away what it represents.

I thought she didn't know. I thought she was in her room when it happened.

The night I fell down the stairs. I broke my arm. It took months to heal. I know it impacted Gracie in a negative way, but I didn't think she knew. She even put band aids on her Barbies where my shoulder dislocated.

I didn't think she knew what happened. It was the night that Roger lost more than his cool.

It was the first time I was terrified of the man I married.

Suddenly the light above me turns off again.

CHAPTER 35

Roger

I sit in my car and drink coffee, staring at the house. I have the radio on but it's hard to relax.

I don't know if Jeremy Timmons is in his home this time. I don't know if his father is back from the hospital either.

I know Gracie isn't there, but Jeremy could have her somewhere else. When I spot him, I'll follow where he goes.

As more time goes by, I realize that I should perhaps park a little further away from the building. It wouldn't be hard to see me.

Then again, Jeremy doesn't know what I look like.

His father does, though. The last thing I want is to give the man another heart attack.

I don't want to hurt anyone.

I just want Gracie back.

Before I turn on my car, a vehicle pulls up beside me, blocking my view of Jeremy's house. I immediately recognize the driver.

Detective Falls lowers her window, and I reluctantly do the same. "Mr. Bradshaw, what are you doing here?"

"Just going for a drive around the neighborhood," I lie. "You know, looking for my daughter."

"Look somewhere else," she says coldly. "If I have to put a detail at this house to make sure no more trouble comes, I will."

I laugh. "Just ridiculous. Police protecting child predators now."

"Go somewhere else," she repeats. "I won't ask again. I'll be talking to my constables in this area. If they spot you here again, they will arrest you."

"Ridiculous," I repeat.

"The father is going to live, by the way," the detective says, before rolling the window back up.

I breathe in deep. Thank God.

Detective Falls stares at me, her vehicle unmoving. I finally get the hint that she won't leave until I do. I turn on the ignition and begin driving away. I look in my rear-view mirror and see the detective still isn't moving, and I'm sure she's watching me right now as well.

I drive home and when I enter, Sarah's mom is sweeping in the kitchen. Her father sits in his wheelchair in front of our living room television, watching sports.

"Thanks again," I say to my mother-in-law.

"Anything new?"

I shake my head. I can feel a tear forming in my eye and quickly glance away from her. "You guys should just go home for the rest of the night."

She gathers her things and comes back for her husband. As she begins to wheel him outside, I call out to her. "Did you hear anything from Sarah?"

She shakes her head this time. I thank her again for staying at my home all day and she reminds me that if I need anything to let her know.

After they leave, I sit at the kitchen table and try to collect myself. It's been nearly twenty-four hours since

Gracie disappeared. All we've found is her hair ribbon.

Since then, things have only gotten worse. No news is bad news when a child is missing. I began to cry and lower my head.

I strike the kitchen table.

What I did to that old man was wrong. What if he died? My rage is getting the better of me, and yet I'm helpless.

I call Sarah again.

I'm not surprised when I have the same results as before.

My daughter is still missing, and now I don't know where my wife is either.

CHAPTER 36

Annie

I open the door to Gracie's room. My heart sinks when I find her in the corner of the room, curled in a ball, crying.

"Gracie," I say softly. "What's wrong?" She doesn't answer, and I make sure to close the door behind me.

"I was scared," she says between sobs. "I asked for you to come. You didn't. You told me you would."

"Sweet pea," I say. "I'm so sorry. I didn't hear you. Were you up from your nap for some time? How about I make you a yummy snack?"

She continues to cry. I kneel beside her and put my arm around her. "It's okay, sweet pea. Don't worry. You don't have to be afraid anymore."

"I want Mommy," she says.

How can she want Mommy? After what she told me, she should never want to go back to her home.

I think of my own mother. She never let a child go too long without the mother in the room with them.

I thought Sarah would be the last thing Gracie needed.

A woman who let her child be in danger from her husband. A child who's mentally abused. Items thrown at her. The poor thing was traumatized. Not to mention what the husband did to Sarah.

He should be in that small room with his wife. I would love nothing more.

Right now, I have something more important to tend to: a crying child.

"I want my mommy," she repeats.

"Well, your mother is still out and we're going to have our sleepover a little longer, okay? Look!" I say. I take my double-jointed thumb and wiggle it comically out of place. I put my hand behind my back and move it back in place, revealing it to her. "Magic!"

My usual form of entertainment doesn't have the same charm now. Gracie is still crying.

"Can you call my mommy? I want to talk to her."

I take a deep breath. "I'll try and call her, and if she picks up, I'll bring you the phone to talk to her." My lie seems to calm Gracie and she stops sobbing a moment. "And I'll never leave you like that again. I'll stay in the room more and won't leave. When I do, it'll be to get your food, okay? Are you hungry?"

She nods her head. "Uh-huh."

"Well, let me see what I can get for us. But, oh no, how will I cook without my thumb?" I move my double-jointed thumb outward and pop it to the side. Gracie laughs. Her giggles fill my heart with joy. "How can I make food with no thumb? What do I do now?"

"You still have that one," she says, pointing at my left thumb.

"Yes! Of course!" I say with great enthusiasm. "I still have this thumb— Oh no." I move it into an awkward position. "This is going to be hard now. Now I have no thumbs!" Gracie is now full-on laughing and I join her. I put my hands behind my back and put both thumbs back

167

to their proper places. "Magic!" I shout when I show her.

She laughs again and I pat her head, telling her I'll be back soon. "How about you watch a movie while we have a snack?" She nods. "Okay, sweet pea." I put on cartoons before leaving the room and locking the door. When I'm in the short hallway, I smile when I look at the other locked room.

As if on cue, I hear the faint sounds of yelling followed by hollow kicks against the door. I shouldn't give her food, I think. She doesn't deserve it. She doesn't deserve anything. Not after what she put Gracie through.

I think of my own mother. She would never do this to a woman who she couldn't confirm was an abuser.

I'm not my mother, though.

I head upstairs and pick a sharp knife from the drawer. I run my hand against the blade before grabbing some vegetables from the fridge. I fix a plate for Gracie and myself. The baby monitor is red, and I can hear the cartoons Gracie is watching.

After a moment I hear her sweet voice. I recognize her tone well. She's playing with a few toys, giving them their unique voices. I smile when I hear her say my name.

"Hi, it's me, Ms. Meadows," Gracie says in a funny voice.

"Hey, Ms. Meadows!" she says, higher.

"Hey, Mommy," the Ms. Meadows voice says. "Can Gracie come over and play?"

"Oh, yes! She would love to. But I want to come too."

"Yeah!" the Ms. Meadows voice says. "We can have fun together."

"I miss Gracie," she says with her pretend mother's voice. "I never want to leave her."

I walk over to the baby monitor and slowly turn it

off, shoving it in the drawer. Lowering my head, I take a moment to myself before walking down the stairs slowly, bringing the snack I've prepared for me and Gracie.

Once in the basement, I hesitate before entering Gracie's room. I place one of the plastic plates down and open the slot to Sarah's. I don't say a word as I place the food inside.

"Annie!" Sarah calls out to me.

Don't talk to them, I remind myself. It was Mother's rule. Although I haven't been very good with following many of them so far on my own.

"Annie, I understand why you did this," she says, this time not yelling. "You think I hurt my child. You think I would hurt Gracie? I would never. I've never touched her in that way. Yes, I've yelled at her, but as a parent, sometimes you have to."

"And Roger!" I shout at the open slot. "What about your husband?"

"He didn't mean to scare her," Sarah says. "He never hurt her, ever."

"And you? How many times has your husband hurt you?"

Sarah doesn't answer.

"You think your husband won't ever touch Gracie, but you probably thought the same until he touched you."

"That was—"

"Another accident?" I yell. "Every terrible thing he's done to you was always one of those, wasn't it? How many excuses will you make for your husband before you realize it's just who he is?"

Sarah's quiet a moment. "His father died. He's not himself."

"My mother's dying!" I shout.

She's quiet again. "I'm sorry... Everyone needs their mother. You understand that. Gracie needs hers."

"It should be your husband in this room," I say coldly. "You deserve each other. He hurts you and you put up with it. My mother was stupid once. She let my father hit her. She told herself the same excuses you told yourself. She said he was a good man. Said he loved her. Said he was a good person."

"He is a good per—"

"Shut up!" I shout. "He's not. He should be the one rotting in this room. He broke your arm, on purpose! Shoved you down the stairs. Gracie told me everything." Sarah is quiet now. "That's right. He's the bad guy here, not me... My father was the bad guy, too. One night, after I behaved poorly, he turned his anger towards me. That's when Mother had enough. She lured him to the room you're in now. They say you can live without food or water for up to eight days. Father died after three... He deserved it."

"Are you going to kill me?" Sarah asks, her voice trembling.

I sigh. "I shouldn't be talking to you." I close the slot and lock it. I'm about to turn and leave towards Gracie's room when I pause. I reluctantly turn on the light in Sarah's room.

CHAPTER 37

Roger

It's starting to get dark out now, and Sarah hasn't returned home. I'm more than worried now. I've called Detective Falls and she said she would radio her officers to look out for her.

How does this happen? Not only is my daughter missing, but so is my wife.

I think about putting out more missing person posters but feel like giving up. I sit on the couch, drinking a beer. It's my fourth. I don't plan on stopping anytime soon. I joke to myself that once Sarah walks in the door, I'll stop drinking.

Until then this is her fault. Why hasn't she returned home? How could she be out for so long without telling me where she is?

I think of how obsessed she was with Annie Meadows. I told Detective Falls that. I take out my phone and out of desperation make a call. This time someone answers.

"Mr. Bradshaw?" the private investigator asks.

I laugh. "Hey. Surprised you picked up."

"PIs work odd hours," he says with a laugh of his own. "What's up?"

"I need another address from you. I need it right

away, too."

"I'm sort of working on something right now. I'm out. I can get it to you in the morning."

I take a long sip from my beer. "No, you don't get it. I think— I'm worried."

There's a pause on the phone. "I know who you are," the PI says. "Do you think this person has your daughter?"

"My wife does," I say. "And now she's missing too." There's a pause on the phone. "Look, I'll pay you triple what I did last time, okay? I just really need this."

"What's the name?"

CHAPTER 38

Sarah

I pace around the small room. Even though I can now see, I can't eat the food Annie made. The last thing I want is to eat. My stomach is empty but so is my heart.

Gracie is only a few feet away from me, and yet I can't see her. I know she's safe, and that makes a huge difference.

I don't know what Annie Meadows has in mind for me, though.

It seems she and her mother have done terrible things, many of them in this room.

Annie's father was killed here.

Her mother locked him in the room until he died from starvation or dehydration. That's what Annie said.

Annie said a lot of things, and some of those words stung. Roger is a good man. He would do anything for his family. He's funny. He's caring. He provides for us.

I start to think of the other things he's done or demanded of me.

He didn't want me working, I remind myself. He didn't want me going out with friends. Any time I did, he would guilt me into staying home. Sometimes he would even pit me against them. I remember wondering why all my friends hated Roger. They didn't see how great of a man he was. They didn't see him the way I did.

They did hear about the fights we had when I told them at work. I told them the bad names he called me. I told them the things he would throw across the room when he was furious with me. I told them it only happened when he was really upset, though. He never physically hurt me.

Scared me, yes, but never hurt me.

Until he did.

I told Roger I wanted to go back to work. I missed being around people. All I had in my life was my husband, mother, and Gracie. I needed more. He told me I didn't have to worry about money. He would take care of it.

I told him I was going to call my old boss. We could easily pay for childcare if I was working. Gracie needed more time with other children. I felt she was becoming too shy, like I was.

I was worried that whatever depression I had, she was picking up on, and as a result of my unhappiness, my little girl was feeling the same.

I needed change.

Roger didn't understand that. He pounded his fist on a table, but this time I wouldn't let him have his way. I stood up in defiance and walked past the stairs. As I did, Roger stood up as well. Next thing I knew, I felt a hard shove and fell down the steps into the basement.

I cried out in pain and Roger immediately ran to me. I saw Gracie at the top of the stairs looking down at me. I hoped she heard my screams and that's why she was there. Now I know from Annie that she saw it happen.

She saw what Roger did.

All through my recovery, Roger treated me nicely. Eventually he said it would be okay if I wanted to go back to work. He even agreed to put Gracie in daycare. He agreed to therapy. He agreed to many things.

I feared my husband but told myself it was a mistake. He was heated in the moment. I yelled at him; I shouldn't have.

I'm not sure why I did it, being as scared as I was. Maybe it was because I felt like I had nothing happening in my life.

My arm eventually healed, but my soul never did.

How many lies have I told to protect my husband and what he did to me? Every doctor's visit I had following my dislocated shoulder, I told lies. I kept my secret. All to protect him.

Every time I sat in that doctor's office and stared at the poster in the waiting room: Report Domestic Abuse.

Every time, I read that poster, but I never said a word to anyone. What's the point? What happens if I do? Would the police do anything about it? What would Roger do if I did?

Roger would leave me. I'd be left by myself to care for a young child. I'm not sure I could do that alone.

Maybe Annie's right about my husband.

What Roger did was wrong. After he nearly hit Gracie with the plate, I started making more excuses for him. He wasn't trying to hurt my child.

How much longer before Roger's temper flares high enough that he has another "accident", hurting Gracie?

The slot at the bottom of the door opens. "I'm going to open the door now," Annie says. "Please stand back. Please don't try anything."

"Okay," I say breathless. "I promise I won't."

She does as she says and slowly opens the door wide. She looks down at my plate of vegetables. "You didn't eat.

You should."

"Can I see Gracie?" I ask.

She keeps one hand outside the door and suddenly puts it behind her back. For a quick moment, I see light reflect off the knife she's hiding.

"Are you going to hurt me?" I ask.

She shakes her head. "Mother had a rule. Never hurt someone who isn't an abuser. I know you're not. Even though your husband is, you're not." She takes a deep breath. "I'm supposed to teach you that your husband is not going to change. You're supposed to realize that."

I lower my head. "He's done some terrible things. You're right." I bend down and grab the picture Gracie made.

Annie steps towards me and quickly takes it from me, placing the drawing on a side table in the hallway. "And yet you don't want to do anything about it, right? If I let you and Gracie leave here, you'll go right back to him, won't you?"

I don't answer, and for a moment, I see Annie shuffle the knife behind her back, changing her grip on the handle.

"Let's go," she says.

"Where?" I say, confused. I almost want her to close the door again.

"Gracie keeps asking for you," she whispers. "She wants her mother. You can come out. I won't hurt you unless you try to hurt me."

"I won't," I promise. "I just need to see her." Annie stands back and gestures for me to leave the room. I shuffle forward until I'm finally out of the room. I wait for Annie to stop hiding the knife and use it on me, but she doesn't.

"Take the piece of wood off the door and go inside. Your daughter's waiting for you."

I smile and tears begin to fill my eyes. Before I open the door, Annie puts a hand on it, stopping me. "I want you to know that I did this to save her. To make her pure again."

"Pure?"

Annie has tears of her own now forming. "What they do to us hurts. It hurts for a lifetime. It never goes away. No matter how much you cry, how much you pray, the pain always stays. What my mother did helped. What she did for other women and children helped. The bad people were destroyed. Vanquished. Defeated. Bad would be defeated by good." Annie takes the knife and puts it at her side, banging it against her upper thigh.

"I'm sorry," I say. For a moment I stare at the young woman in front of me. The trauma that she's been hiding with her wide smiles is visible now. I can't help but think of Gracie when I look at her.

I never want what Roger does to make her this way.

"Thank you," I say to her. I'm not sure why I say it. It makes no sense. At first I think it's because she's letting me leave the room and see Gracie, but I wonder if it's for something else.

Annie smiles at me and opens the door. "I'll be locking it behind you."

CHAPTER 39
Annie

I take the knife and stab it downward into the kitchen table, watching with amazement as it stays in place. I lower my head into my hands.

No matter what I did, Gracie wanted her mother. No matter how much I played with her. No matter how many games we played, the laughs I gave her, she wanted to see Sarah.

I'm not her mother.

I took her to protect her from the bad, and that's not Sarah. It's her husband. I grind my teeth thinking of him. I should have never taken Gracie.

It was impulsive. Not planned. It went against every rule Mother had. The past few days I haven't been myself. I know it's because Mother is dying.

Part of me can understand Roger Bradshaw through this.

I walk over to the drawer and take out the baby monitor, turning it on. A light on the device turns red and I can hear them downstairs.

"Mommy!" Gracie says, laughing. "Stop kissing me!"

"I can't stop!" I can suddenly hear her kissing her as if I'm in the room with them. "Oh my, I just missed you so much."

"I just had a sleepover with Ms. Meadows. Just like I have with Grandma. It was only one sleep, and I was gone."

Sarah laughs. "Yeah, I guess that's right. I just—"

"Mommy. You're hugging too tight." I hear the audible kisses again. "Mommy, your spit is all over me."

I smile a moment, listening to them. I think of my own mother.

What do I do with Sarah? What should I do with Gracie? I never had a plan. I just wanted to help the child. I acted impulsively.

"Are you hurt, Gracie? Did Ms. Meadows do anything bad?"

"No, Mommy. We had fun. Read books and did crafts. She didn't let me have chocolate, though."

Sarah laughs. "Is this a new dress?"

"Yeah!" Gracie says. "Ms. Meadows made it for me. It has ladybugs on it. See?"

The phone on the kitchen wall rings loudly. I listen to Gracie and Sarah a moment before lowering the sound on the baby monitor.

"Hello," I say, picking up the phone. "Meadows' residence. This is Annie." I'm not sure why I greet a caller this way. I'm the only one in the house now.

"Annie," a voice says, "it's Melanie, your mother's nurse."

"Oh, hey," I say. My heart stops beating. "Is everything okay?"

"I'm so sorry," she says. "She passed about an hour ago."

"Mother?" I ask surprised. I know she's talking about her, and I expected this moment, but now that it's here, it hits me differently.

"Yes, your mother has died... I'm so sorry."

I let her words sink in and take a moment to compose myself. "Thank you for calling," I say before hanging up.

"Mommy," I hear Gracie's voice say through the baby monitor.

"Yes, dear?"

"I love you, Mommy."

"I love you too, honey."

I pick up the baby monitor and slowly lower the volume until it turns off. A moment of rage hits me and I whip it into the living room and watch it break into pieces across the floor.

"No!" I shout. "No!" I bury my head in my hands again. "Mother. Why?" I cover my face in disbelief. The hard truth of my life hits me. "I'm alone now." Tears roll down my face. "You left me here."

I look at the mess I made in the living room. I open the closet by the front door, take out a broom, and sweep up some of the broken pieces of the baby monitor while trying my best to not break down. After cleaning the mess, instead of picking it up with the dustpan, I throw the broom to the floor.

"You left me here," I say to no one.

Outside, I see a man in a grey sweater walking along the sidewalk. I immediately recognize his crooked nose.

The child abuser.

Another bad man. One that walks free even after the things he's done. Even though I don't know what he did, it was enough to be on a list of known predators.

He's the worst kind of bad man. One that hurts children and likes it.

Where's this bad man heading to now?

I quickly go to the kitchen. It takes some force for me

to remove the knife from the table. I put on my shoes and leave my house and walk in his direction. I follow him, trying my best to not make it obvious, but at one point, he glances back at me and gives me a strange look.

I smile back and conceal the knife behind me.

It's nighttime now. I'm a young woman following a very bad man. I'm the one who's supposed to be afraid.

I'm not.

I need to wait, though. Mother had rules. I may not follow them well, and tend to make my own, but she had an important one.

Make sure the bad men are bad.

The predator turns down a street, and I know where he's going. After several more minutes, he sits on a park bench, looking at a playground. It's dark now, and no children are outside playing.

I've seen him do this before, though, in the light of day. Near the daycare.

I watch him as he sits. I conceal myself behind a large tree, every so often peeking around to look at what he's doing. It doesn't take long for him to stand up and start walking back towards me.

I wait until he's close enough to greet him. When he passes the tree, I show myself with a wide smile.

"Magic," I say loudly.

Before he can say a word, I whip my hand and the knife across his neck. His skin opens and blood gushes from his body. He immediately falls to the ground.

I stand over him and watch until the bad man takes his last breath.

CHAPTER 40

Annie

Adrenaline runs through my body and I'm breathing rapidly.

My hand is still shaking. The other is holding the bloody knife, steady.

I never wanted to kill someone. That was what I told myself when I took Gracie. I thought my mother was wrong for killing. I thought there was a better way to save a child.

After killing the predator, I know I was wrong. Wrong about everything.

Mother too.

Why save only one child? Imagine the number of children I saved from years of trauma by killing that man.

I'm astounded by myself. I feel no shame for my action. It seems right. If there is a pure evil in this world, that predator was it. Now he's gone.

Good defeated evil.

I saved children tonight.

It was only a matter of time before that man did more in the playground than watch the children.

Now he will never hurt anyone.

The best part, he won't be my last. At the daycare,

there's a whole bulletin board of evil men who can each be given a similar fate.

No need to keep them in a locked room, starving them to death. Murder them where you find them. Move on to the next.

After all, there's so many.

If I was to purify the city of the men on the list at work, people would thank me.

Who cries over such a human being?

I look at the knife in my hand and try to calm my breathing. Blood drips from the tip onto the floor.

My heart is still beating fast. I feel like I've had ten espressos. I almost want to go to the daycare and start looking into the next monster on the list.

The only thing that stops me is the two people in my basement. What do I do with Sarah?

What do I do with Roger Bradshaw? I look at the knife in my hand and grip the handle tighter.

The answer is obvious now.

I wanted to save Gracie. There's only one way to do that.

I head down the stairs, the bloody knife still in my hand. I unlock the door and pop my head inside.

"Sarah," I say in a soft voice. I give her a wide smile. "Can we talk, please? Out in the hall?"

Sarah looks at me with concern. She kisses Gracie on the head before she stands up from the couch. She reluctantly walks towards the door. I wave at her to hurry.

When she's outside the room, I close the door.

"I've given this some thought," I say, although I'm not sure if I can think at all right now. With the jitters in my body, I could run a marathon at the moment. Sarah covers her mouth and screams into her hand.

"Stop!" I shout back. "You're going to scare Gracie."

Sarah looks at me in complete horror.

I know I've scared her, but I'm about to let her go with an important caveat that she must agree to.

You think she would be happier about it instead of looking at me like I'm a ghost.

"Sarah, what's wrong?" I say, utterly confused.

She removes the hand from her mouth. "You're covered in blood."

CHAPTER 41

Roger

The private investigator came through for me. He provided Annie's address quickly.

For the second time today, I'm driving to a house and I have no clue what I'll do when I get there. The last thing I want is to put Annie Meadows through what I did to Jeremy's father.

Although Detective Falls told me he'll survive, I still can't let go of what my actions had done to the man.

When I get to Annie's house it'll be different.

After all, Annie is a stick of a woman. I can't just barrel into her home, even though it'd be very easy to do. I easily have fifty pounds on her.

The way Gracie talks about the woman, you would think she's a second mother. Gracie seems to genuinely like her daycare teacher.

In what world would it make sense that Annie took her?

I still believe in my heart Jeremy's behind everything. I need to find Sarah, and then I'll go back to focusing on the pervert. I'll tail him. Anywhere he goes, I'll be there.

To hell with Detective Falls.

If I have to, I'll rent a car. I need to get better at

following people. I thought about hiring the PI I've used to watch Jeremy. If the pervert has Gracie, though, I don't want to involve anyone else in what I may do.

As I get closer to Annie Meadows' home, I slow until I spot her address. I park on the street. Again, I don't have a plan. I'll knock on the front door. What else should I do?

I'm never going to break into a home again. Not after the old man. I don't want to scare a petite woman like Annie Meadows. Her and Jeremy's father could be sharing a hospital room in the ER if I do.

I walk up the stairs to her front door. When I reach the porch, I step in something slippery, nearly causing me to fall. I look down but can't make out what it was. When I take another step an automatic light pops on, illuminating me and the porch.

I already see a light on inside and know she must be home. There's a good chance she's seen me already.

I'm about to knock on the door, when I look down and see what caused me to nearly fall.

Bloody footprints start past the porch steps and lead to the front door.

"What the hell?" I peer through the window but don't see any movement.

Something's very wrong. Whose blood did I step in?

I peer through the other windows on the front porch but see nothing. I see a basement window below the porch with a light on. Something is blocking me from seeing completely into the room, though.

I kneel on the pavement and try my best to look inside. When I do, I'm in complete shock.

Sarah has her mouth covered. Beside her is Annie Meadows. The daycare teacher's white dress is covered in red stains. In her hand is a large kitchen knife.

I immediately run to the front door again. When I turn the knob, it opens.

CHAPTER 42

Sarah

"Whose blood is that?" I say, pointing at Annie.

She smiles. "It belonged to a bad man. A very bad man."

I cover my mouth again. "Did you kill him? Roger?"

She sighs. "You still care for him? How? After everything you told me. How little he cares for you." She points the knife at me. When I take a step back, she softens her expression. "Sorry." She turns it away again.

"He's done terrible things, yes, but I don't want him to die."

She shakes her head. "No, silly. I'll do that for you." Her dead eyes make her look almost demonic. "That's what I wanted to tell you. This ends with him. Roger 'it was an accident' Bradshaw. I'll kill him," she says, whipping the knife through the air, "and then you leave." She laughs. "It'll be just like Mother would have wanted."

Annie suddenly lowers her knife after mentioning her mother.

"No, Annie, you can't do that to him," I say.

Her eyes harden, and she stares at me intensely. "Why not? He doesn't deserve you. He certainly doesn't deserve Gracie. If I let you leave, you'll just go right back to him. You won't have learned anything!"

"What your father did to you was terrible. But killing won't make it better. It hasn't made it better for you, has it?"

She pauses a moment before raising the blade towards me. Just then Gracie opens the door slightly. "Mommy, are you coming back?" she asks.

I close the door, trying to not hit her with it. There's no way I can let her see what's happening, or the blood all over her daycare teacher.

"Wait inside, honey," I tell her. I look at Annie Meadows and worry this may be the last time I talk to my daughter. "Gracie," I open the door slightly to look at her sweet face. She turns to me. "I love you. Mommy loves you so much. Always remember that, no matter what."

Gracie smiles back. "You're silly, Mommy. You keep saying you love me."

I close the door and look at Annie. "Just don't hurt her, okay?" I cover my mouth again and wait in terror for her to stick the blade into me.

When I look at Annie, her rage filled eyes have softened. The knife has lowered, and she looks on the brink of tears.

"I lost her today," she says suddenly. "Mother. She died." I breathe in deep. Annie turns the knife in her hand so she's holding it by the tip. "Here," she says. "Take it. Please, take it."

I take the knife quickly. Blood from the handle now stains my hands.

What she says next terrifies me.

"Kill me," she says softly. "Please? Let me be with Mother. I'm not meant for this anymore. I should never have taken Gracie. I should have never done that to her. I should never have put you through this. I should never have helped Mother with any of the children. I should have never been alive to begin with... Kill me."

"Annie, stop,"

She begins to cry and lowers her head. "I just didn't want that little girl to go through what I did. I didn't want her to be broken. Look what it's done to me. I would do anything to stop her from being hurt. None of them deserved to be hurt." She lowers her head and sobs uncontrollably. It almost reminds me of how Gracie looks when she's sad.

I'm not sure what it is. The woman in front of me is covered in blood. I just took a knife from her. But despite that, I feel for her.

I never wanted my little girl to be broken either. For the first time, I've realized I've been *broken* for a while.

In a weird way, Annie Meadows has saved me.

I drop the knife and take a step towards her. "It's okay, Annie." I wrap my arms around her and hug her tight.

"I miss my mother," she says, weeping into my shoulder. "I wish none of this had happened."

"It's going to be okay, Annie," I tell her. "Gracie will never be broken. She has her mother to keep her safe from now on. You don't have to worry. I understand why you did this."

When I look up, I see Roger sneaking up behind her.

Before I can say a word, he jumps towards us. He shoves Annie hard. I watch as the young woman falls, her head banging hard against the side table. Roger stands over top of her and throws a vicious punch into her side.

I push my husband and yell for him to stop. He shoves

me as well and my face smashes into the concrete wall. I scream from the pain.

Roger doesn't stop his attack on Annie.

"Roger!" I yell. "Stop, now."

He finally turns to me, his eyes full of rage. "What the hell are you doing?"

"Stop hurting her!" I say. He takes a step towards me, and for a split second, I fear what he'll do next. I point to the room. "Gracie's there!"

Rogers eyes soften and he immediately runs over to the door and attempts to open it.

I stare at Annie Meadows on the floor. She's not moving. A pool of blood is growing wider from under her head.

I realize she's dead.

She's with her mother now.

I look at Roger with rage-filled eyes of my own.

My husband finally opens the door and steps inside the dark room. "Where's the light?" he demands. I turn it on from outside. He looks around and back at me, confused. "Where's Gracie?"

Instead of answering him, I slam the door and lock it from the outside.

CHAPTER 43

Roger

I yell as loudly as I can. "Sarah! Open the door! Open it now! What the hell are you doing?" I start kicking it furiously. When I don't hear her, I start ramming my body into the door. It doesn't budge an inch. I take a step back and kick it as hard as I can, but all I do is injure myself.

"Sarah! Open this door now! Or else!"

I hear a metallic sound and look down, seeing a metal flap open.

"I'm not supposed to talk to you," Sarah says to me coldly.

"What the hell does that mean? What are you doing? What's gotten into you?"

Suddenly a piece of paper slides through the opening. The metal slot closes. I try pushing on it, but it won't nudge. I take a deep breath and grab the piece of paper.

On it is a stick figure at the top of a staircase. At the bottom are two stick figures with frowning faces. "Sarah?" I say, confused. "Is this from Gracie? Is this us?" I look at the stick figure at the top of the stairs and realize who it is.

The light above me turns off.

CHAPTER 44

Sarah

"Remember what I said, honey," I tell Gracie.

She nods. "No peeking."

"That's right," I tell her. I lower the pillowcase I took from her bed and cover her eyes. I tighten it behind her head, so she won't be able to see what's beyond the door. "And what else?"

Gracie covers her ears. "Earmuffs!"

I take one of her hands off her ears for a moment. "That's right. Now, promise me you won't take your hands off your ears." Gracie again agrees.

When I feel comfortable enough to believe her, and to face what's outside the room myself, I open the door. I take Gracie's hand and guide her out. I take a moment to look at Annie Meadows, her body still not moving.

At the end of the hall, I hear the faint sounds of my husband shouting, and him ramming against the door. I take a deep breath and continue to guide Gracie along the hallway and up the stairs. I take off her blindfold once we're on the main floor.

"Time to leave," I tell her.

"Can I sleep over at Ms. Meadows' again sometime?" she asks innocently.

I look at her, unsure what to say. "Let's just go."

"Where are we going now, Mommy?"

I know exactly where we're going, but I don't tell her. I open the front door and take in the fresh air. It's nearly pitch dark outside.

The porch light turns on with our movement and in horror I notice the blood at my feet.

"Somebody made a mess with their paint, Mommy," Gracie says.

I grab her hand. "That's right, honey. Come on now. Let's leave."

We walk a few blocks until I see the sign of the city police station. My pulse quickens as I open the front door and walk inside. An officer gives me a strange look as I walk up to his desk.

"Can, uh, I help you?" he asks.

I stare at the officer, unsure what to say. Yes, I do need help. A lot of help. Where do I start, though?

Annie Meadows is dead. My husband killed her. Annie killed someone else tonight as well. My daughter was taken, and so was I.

So many things I could say, but still, I can't find the words to tell the officer.

"Ma'am," he says, confused. "Are you okay? Is everything alright?" Suddenly the expression on his face changes. He looks over at a missing person poster on a bulletin board near him. Gracie's face is on it. He looks back at me with realization now of who me and my daughter are.

How do I tell him what happened? Where do I start? I think of the doctor's office and the poster that I stared at with contempt for months as my shoulder recovered.

The beginning. You always tell a story from the beginning.

I look at the officer confidently now. "I need to report my husband for abuse."

Epilogue
Annie

I wake up in a small room. Instantly I feel pain in my head. I cover my head to make it stop and feel a large bandage around my skull.

I look around the room in disbelief. A machine beside me is beeping. I try to raise my other hand, but something is stopping me. I look down in disbelief.

Handcuffs. One around my hand, the other the bed.

A hospital bed.

What happened? How did I end up here? The last thing I remember was talking to Sarah Bradshaw, and next thing I see is this hospital room.

How did I end up here?

I tug on the cuffs, but can't free myself. In my other arm I see tubes running from the top of my hand. I reach across my body and pull them out.

Before I can do anything else, a nurse walks into the room. Her mouth gapes open when she sees me staring back at her. She immediately runs out, and I hear her jogging along the hospital hallway.

I tug at my handcuffed hand again, unable to free myself. I take a deep breath and smile. I jolt my thumb inside the palm of my hand and slide the handcuffs off.

"Magic."

* * *

Note from the author:

I truly hope you enjoyed reading my story as much as I did creating it. As an indie author, what you think of my book is all I care about.

If you enjoyed my story, please take a moment to leave your review on the Amazon store. It would mean the world to me.

Thank you for reading, and I hope you join me next time.

Download My Free Book

If you would like to receive a FREE copy of my psychological thriller, The Affair, please email me at jamescaineauthor@gmail.com.

I'm always happy to receive emails from readers at jamescaineauthor@gmail.com.

Thanks again,
James

And now please enjoy a short excerpt from my book, *The Boss.*

THE BOSS

**I have my dream job,
With a nightmare boss.**

At first, Nicole Barret seemed to be the perfect boss.

I was dead wrong.

It gets worse when I find out my husband knows her all too well. She's his ex-fiancé.

She won't let me quit without destroying my career and my marriage.

It wasn't a coincidence that she hired me.

It won't be a coincidence if I disappear.

The Boss is a page-turning psychological thriller filled with twists, suspense and mind-blowing tension, from James Caine, the author of The In-Laws and The Family Cabin.

Please enjoy this sneak preview of The Boss:

PROLOGUE

A good boss doesn't kill their staff.

I stand by the sink, looking at the red stains on my pants suit, blood splattered on my face. I run the faucet, letting the sound of the gushing water mesmerize me.

What had I just done?

This went too far.

It was stupid, I know. It wasn't my fault, though. I take a paper towel and wipe away the blood from my forehead.

What I have done will change everything. Jail is not an option, though.

I look at myself in the mirror, my face nearly clean of the blood. How pathetic do I look? How scared do I seem?

This is not me. I'm confident, overconfident at that. I'm a businesswoman. I exude power. The people who work for me expect me to lead them as I always have. I'm more than respected at the office. People are afraid to be near me.

Not because I'm scary, but because I expect the best out of my staff. I expect the best because I give the best effort, and others need to show me they will do the same.

That's the attitude that made me climb the corporate ladder at Lovely Beauty Supplies to become president, after all. Executives in Toronto know me. I'm a leader amongst a group of leaders.

I'm Nicole Barrett, dammit. A natural leader. A boss that people can not only look up to but strive to be. I've not only made it to the top of the food chain of Toronto's executive elite, I'm at the forefront.

Me. A woman who came from nothing. I became everything, and at the age of thirty-one.

You don't get to where I am by being weak or lazy. I put in my time every day to be the best, until I was just that.

I regard the pathetic little girl in the mirror who looks scared at the actions she just committed.

This person doesn't show confidence, only fear. This little girl looks like a scared poor child living in squalor with her mother, not a president of a major commercial beauty company.

I hate the little girl staring back at me from the mirror.

I put my hands under the water and find relief in my clean hands, while watching the red go down the drain, taking in a deep breath.

Everything will change now. I look back at the dead body staining the tile floor behind me.

This was not my fault.

It was Alice Walker's fault.

I should have never hired her to begin with.

CHAPTER 1

Alice
Three months prior.

I sit on the couch in our new living room, paralyzed with fear of all the major changes in my life.

I know I should be happy right now. I'm getting everything I ever wanted. Instead, my insecurities have completely taken over my brain. I'm stuck between a feeling of jumping up and down with joy and wanting to curl up in a ball and cry.

Tomorrow is my first day at a Lovely Beauty Supplies, or LBS for short. I'm their new executive director of sales.

My jaw still drops to the floor when I think of my new title.

It took me years to get into a management role when I lived in British Columbia. Next thing I know, I've moved across the country and now I'm a few inches away from being a top executive in an emerging beauty supply company that has huge potential.

Hard work brought me here. I paid my dues to my corporate bosses. I sacrificed a lot of my time and life to get to where I wanted to be, and now the fruits of my labor are paying off.

Evan, my husband, has been supportive of me. He hasn't slowed me down in what I wanted in life, although he can be a good distraction.

We're nearly thirty. He wants to be a father. When we married nearly two years ago, I told him I wanted the same, and I do – but not right now.

Right now, Alice Walker needs to focus on herself. I need to climb the corporate ladder as high as I can go, and once I'm invaluable, once I've proven my worth, I can focus on having a family with Evan.

I'm young and still have plenty of time. Although Evan seems to be going through his midlife crisis much earlier than expected, I'm only twenty-seven. That allows me a lot of time to get to where I need to be.

If you ask Evan, though, he would tell you otherwise. He is obsessed with my eggs and how many of my child rearing years I have left.

He will continue to sneak in statistics of issues older parents have when they have a family later in life.

I'm not worried. When the time comes, I'll make a good mother, I know. I just can't start when I'm at the bottom. I want my children to be raised in an environment where they don't have to worry about money. I want to ensure that I can provide those stable early years for them.

Essentially, I want them to not go through the hell I had growing up.

Evan, while being a good, supportive husband to his overachieving wife, doesn't really help much in that department.

He's currently not working, and that's okay since we just moved to Toronto so that I could start my new job.

Although I tend to set high expectations for myself, I know it's not reasonable for him to move across the country with me and suddenly find work.

What was reasonable, though, was to expect that before we moved to Toronto, he would have a stable career. *Stable* and *career* are not words that are relevant to my husband.

In the working world, we are near opposites. I'm a go-getter, overachiever and will do anything except sell my unborn child to move myself to where I want to be in life. Evan is different.

He won't take any garbage from his superiors. He puts in the work that's required of him and barely anything extra. He gloats about how he quit his last job by telling his boss a four-letter word that starts with F.

Sometimes I can tell he's upset about how successful I am. I never shove it in his face that I make more than him. He knows it. We do our finances together. He sees what I make compared to what he brings in, when he has a job. I don't have to tell him the obvious.

I make enough that he doesn't have to worry about it. I know that a lot of his frustration at the various jobs he's had is that he hasn't found something he's passionate about.

Since I was a girl, I wanted to be an executive at a company. I imagined my name on the outside of a large door in a fancy office, staff working for me, and me leading them.

At one point in his life, I thought Evan had that. He was starting his Bachelors of Education to become a teacher, but dropped out of university in his early twenties. He's struggled to find something he wants to do since.

If he really wants to have a family with me, and with me making more than him, he will likely be the one at home with our future baby more than me. I'll have to return to work early from maternity leave to focus on my career again. He can take on the brunt of what the baby needs.

'You want me to be Mr. Mommy?' Evan asked me once as a joke.

Evan comes up the stairs from the basement, each step squeaking in different tones. He has cut wires in his hand.

"Well, this is a mess," he says. "The electrical wiring is straight out of the 1940s. This wouldn't meet code for sure." He looks at me, waiting for a response, but I just grin.

We knew this place was more than a fixer upper.

Evan found an amazing opportunity, he called it. An older house listed online with an incredible price in a nice area.

The description was nice and fluffy as you would expect. Saying a house is expensive in Toronto is an understatement. This is the most expensive city to live in Canada, even the world for that matter.

We had always wanted a home, and if we were to have a baby sometime in the near future, we wanted to have one in a detached house.

Evan smiles back. "Don't worry, I can handle it," he says confidently.

Although my husband is not confident in the regular workplace, he is certainly handy. His father worked in maintenance and taught his son many different things, from installing flooring even to electrics.

It was something the Walker family would do together. Any house project that was needed to be done, his father would round up Evan and youngest son, Tommy, and they would do it together.

When I got the job at LBS, Evan was happy he would be moving back to where he was raised. He would be close to his brother Tommy again.

Evan's father would have loved working on renovating this place with him, but unfortunately he passed a year ago. Instead of the Walker family working on a house project together, it would only be Evan and Tommy now.

"When is Tommy coming by to help?" I ask.

"He said he wanted to come tomorrow," Evan says, stuffing the cables in a garbage bag. He already piled up a bunch of debris from things he tore out. Tommy has a truck they can put it in to bring to the dump. "He said he had a few last things he had to do at school before his summer vacation could really begin." He wipes his dirty hands on his jeans.

"Have to love the life of a teacher," I say with a laugh, and immediately regret my words. Sometimes,

Evan can be sensitive talking about his brother being a teacher. After all, it was his dream job that he gave up on while his brother succeeded.

"What are you looking at?" Evan asks, nodding at my phone.

"The website of my new company. Lovely Beauty Supplies."

"You're already hired there," Evan says with a chuckle. "You don't have to worry about the company's motto now that the interviews are over. You got the job."

Evan doesn't understand. Your job doesn't end with the interview. It starts the first day, and the next. You need to understand the company's work dynamic, what they want. It's the only way to stay at the top or climb even higher at a company.

The work culture you can learn once you're at the office, but understanding your company, at least the public face of it, is important. At the moment, though, I'm reading the company's About Us page and looking at the numerous faces of corporate positions and who's in them.

One of them I immediately knew. She was the one who hired me. Nicole Barrett. I had never interviewed with the president of a company before and was nervous, but she was extremely friendly, which made it go well.

What made it even better was the amount of preparation I had done before the interview started. Nicole even commented on how well-prepared I was.

I smile at my husband. "I need to refresh what I learned from before. Tomorrow is the first day, and you only have one good chance at first impressions."

"I thought you said your boss seemed nice," he says, confused.

"Well, she is, but it's not just her I need to impress, it's everyone."

Evan turns his head to the side. "You'll be fine."

"I know," I say confidently. "That's why I'm preparing some more."

Evan nods. "You say you'll be fine, but you're doing

that thing you do when you're freaking out inside but trying to not show it."

"What?" I say, confused.

"It's your only poker tell I've noticed." He laughs. "If it wasn't for you flaring your nostrils like you're trying to breathe in all the air in the room at once, I would never suspect a thing."

I realize immediately he's right and relax my face.

I sigh and put my phone down. Evan sits on the couch beside me, wrapping his arm around me. "You're going to do just fine tomorrow."

I breathe in deep and rest my head on his shoulder. "I hope you're right."

"You'll see," he says. "And, if for some reason you don't, you can quit. Some other company will be lucky to have my successful wife manage them." He kisses the side of my head.

I don't correct him. It's not that easy. If this doesn't go well, we're totally screwed. I don't explain this to him, though. I wish I had his carefree attitude at times.

Evan takes a hand out of his pocket and a small, rectangular piece of paper falls onto the floor. I see an image of a yellow bell on it, and for a moment worry it's a scratch ticket. Evan used to buy many lottery tickets, and much worse, but he promised he gave that up. Now I see a scratch ticket on the floor?

He picks it up and stares at me, noticing how angry I look. He laughs. "It's just a receipt from the hardware store." He flashes it at me, and I can see the bold letters beside the bell symbol. "Bell Hardware," it reads.

"I'll leave you be," he says as he kisses me again before standing up and going back down the stairs, the steps making different creaking sounds from the kind they made when he came up.

I breathe out and put a finger to my neck, feeling my pulse. It's typically fast but beating out of control at the moment. I slow my breathing and try to calm myself.

I look back down at my cell phone and continue to

read the company site, taking in the information about the products they sell and their marketing.

My phone begins to vibrate in my hand from an unknown caller. I accept the call and put it to my ear. "Hello," I say. Nobody answers me. I look at my phone and see the call is still active. I try again to greet whoever called but hang up when no one responds.

Another scammer. I've been getting a lot lately. I have no time for those tonight, though.

I need to absorb as much information as I can before tomorrow.

I need tomorrow to go well.

Please, go well.

I hope the people I'll manage like me. I hope they aren't nasty. I hope my superiors are easy to work with.

I calm myself again with slow breathing. The president of the company, Nicole Barrett, was so pleasant during the interviews, I remind myself. If the rest of the company is anything like her, tomorrow will be amazing. I hope.

CHAPTER 2
Nicole

How could everything go so wrong, so quickly?

I, of course, know the answer, but would rather not think it.

I was on top of the world, a leader amongst the elite. A role model for women. I was in *Forbes* fucking *Magazine*.

Soon, I'll be nothing.

I look around my home. The comforts of my large luxury apartment in downtown Toronto will mean nothing when I'm behind bars. When I looked down at everyone from my tower, I felt like I was on top of the world.

I sigh. What I would do to have someone to lean on at the moment. Someone who could calm me and tell me everything will be fine.

I don't have that, though. I'm completely alone.

I've been so focused on work that my actual friends abandoned me a long time ago. My colleagues that came up with me as executives I brought down a long time ago. They were the competition, after all. I had to get ahead of them.

No husband. No children. No time for either of those.

I swirl an expensive cabernet sauvignon in my wine glass, smelling it before taking another sip. I continue to think about all the life decisions that have led me to where I am now.

If my life were a movie, it would easily be as doomed as the *Titanic*. I scowl as I take another sip, tapping the side of the glass with my long nails.

I top my glass, filling it to the brim, nearly finishing the bottle.

I walk out onto the balcony and stare at the shimmering lights in the darkness. I used to be infatuated with the view. I used to be infatuated with my apartment – my life.

I lean over the edge of the balcony and look directly down. I wonder what would happen if I let go of my glass and let it fall, possibly hitting the little specks of people walking below. I laugh and take a long sip.

I'd give up this lifestyle in a heartbeat now, knowing what's in store for me.

Of course, I only see that now when I may face jail time.

Oh, god, what did I do?

I stare at the full moon, taking in a moment of its beauty before screaming into the darkness. With the sounds of the traffic below and the large metropolis, nobody will really hear me anyway, aside from the older couple who lives on the only other apartment on my floor and the few neighbors below me.

I could shout till my head exploded and nobody would care. I look down from my balcony.

Nobody would care if I jumped either.

The thought scares me, and I step back until I'm inside my bedroom. I slam the patio door behind me, taking another long sip.

I look around at the apartment. The expensive artwork, furniture, fireplace. Everything I own is the best.

I'd give it up now if I could.

All I wanted for the last fifteen years was to be where I am today, and now I wish I wasn't here. I wish I wasn't who I am anymore. Hell, I wish I wasn't alive at times, as sad as that is to think.

I walk down the hallway, past my security camera

aimed at the front door. Several years ago, there was an armed robber who managed to enter the building and cause some issues for the rich tenants that live here. After that, I decided to get my own system.

It calms me knowing that I'm safe if I have to be.

I walk into a smaller room that I sometimes work out of when I'm not feeling well and stay home, which is rare. I keep all my awards, articles on the wall and anything else that praises me in here.

First I look at the *Forbes Magazine.* "Top woman executives of the year," the article reads. On the cover is me. I take a long drink of wine, squinting at it, not recognizing the confident woman looking back at me.

I sit at my desk. On it is the one picture of me as a child. It was when I spent the summer with my aunt at her farmhouse. My mom thought I'd get a kick out of living amongst the sheep and pigs. She thought it would bother me, but I loved it.

I look at my younger self, my long blond hair tied in pig tails that my aunt Thelma showed me how to do. I'm smiling wide inside the barn with a large pig beside me. I laugh as I remember its name. Gertie the pig.

My smile fades when I think how my aunt Thelma is doing today. She moved to a nursing home recently. She's made me the executor of her will for when she eventually passes, which sadly could be soon. I'll have to figure out what to do with Aunt Thelma's run-down house and old blue barn.

Maybe I'll keep it just for nostalgic reasons.

I wonder if Aunt Thelma is happy with how her life has been. She too has no kids or husband. She only had her farm, and yet she seemed to live a much happier life than I ever could have.

I look at the old picture of me again. What I would do to be that little girl and start over.

I would make different decisions, better ones. Ones that wouldn't bring me to where I am today.

Maybe I would have gotten married. Had kids.

Have a *small* life. Be one of those little specks of people that I always look down at from my balcony.

I was in love, a long time ago. The thought of him upsets me, and I take another sip of wine and put my glass on the desk, for a change letting the alcohol out of my hands tonight.

I open a drawer and take out some paperwork I brought from work the day before.

Tomorrow, we have a new hire starting at Lovely Beauty Supplies. A young woman who I scouted out personally.

Her LinkedIn profile was not bad. She had plenty of management and leadership experience.

She's also married with no children. Her husband is unemployed, most of the time. She was born and raised in Vancouver. I'm sure the move to Toronto, away from her friends and family, will be hard.

Her husband, however, his family lives in Ontario.

They bought a house in a nice area, despite how hideous it is. A fixer upper indeed. It was a place that made my aunt's farmhouse look as luxurious as my apartment.

Alice likes her coffee black, with nothing in it. Some say that's a sign that you're a psychopath, but I disagree since that's how I take mine.

I know her home addresses for the past ten years, her husband's as well.

I know many things about Alice Walker, most of which I learned not from our virtual interview. I hired someone good. A company that I've dealt with before. Their top investigator does fantastic work. When I read their reports, I felt like I knew Alice Walker personally instead of reading words from a piece of paper.

I pick up my wine glass and smile before taking a long drink. I finish the glass and wonder if I should open another bottle.

It's a work night, though. I typically limit myself to two glasses a night, not two bottles.

I look at the candid photos the investigator took of Alice Walker. I take my time looking at the ones he took of her husband, Evan.

From the investigator's reporting, I know him well too now.

Alice is about to start her new executive role at LBS. She's probably nervous right now, in her ugly house, with her handsome husband, anxious for tomorrow to come. I would be. This is the opportunity of a lifetime. If she does well, she'll climb the corporate ladder and make a name for herself.

She could even be the next... Well, me.

I laugh again at the absurdity.

If it wasn't for me finding her profile, she would have remained in Vancouver. I'm sure she would have done okay for herself, but my company could truly make her.

Too bad for her it won't.

Her first day at work tomorrow is the first day of the last of her dreams.

I walk down the hallway, waving like a silly child to my security camera when I pass it.

If my life is the *Titanic* and I'm going down, I may as well bring a few others with me.

I stand in front of my wine rack and grab the most expensive bottle. I pop the cork aggressively and drink from the bottle.
